WINTER IS NOT FOREVER

WINTER IS NOT FOREVER

JANETTE OKE

BETHANY HOUSE PUBLISHERS
MINNEAPOLIS, MINNESOTA 55438
A Division of Bethany Fellowship, Inc.

Cover illustration by Dan Thornberg, Bethany House Publishers
staff artist.

Published by Bethany House Publishers
A Division of Bethany Fellowship, Inc.
6820 Auto Club Road, Minneapolis, Minnesota 55438

Printed in the United States of America

Library of Congress Cataloging-in-Publication Data

Oke, Janette, 1935-
   Winter is not forever.

   (Seasons of the heart series ; bk. 3)
   Sequel to: Winds of autumn.
   I. Title. II. Series: Oke, Janette, 1935- .
Seasons of the heart series ; bk. 3.
PR9199.3.038W56 1988   813'.54   88-2882
ISBN 1-55661-002-5 (pbk.)

Dedicated
to the memory of Amanda Janette,
our third grandchild,
daughter of Terry and Barbara, and baby sister of Ashley,
who came to join our family on June 25, 1987,
and completed her brief mission on September 10, 1987,
taken from us suddenly by crib death.

She was such a healthy, happy responsive little
sweetheart!
We loved her dearly and miss her greatly.

And to Amanda's grandparents
Koert and Carol Dieterman
and all readers who have suffered through like pain.
Our loving and faithful God wipes our tears,
mends our broken hearts, and heaven becomes a dearer
place.

"For where the treasure is, there will the heart be also."

JANETTE OKE
PRAIRIE LOVE STORIES

JANETTE OKE was born in Champion, Alberta, during the depression years, to a Canadian prairie farmer and his wife. She is a graduate of Mountain View Bible College in Didsbury, Alberta, where she met her husband, Edward. They were married in May of 1957, and went on to pastor churches in Indiana as well as Calgary and Edmonton, Canada.

Janette's husband is president of Mountain View Bible College, Didsbury, Alberta. The Okes have three sons and one daughter and are enjoying the addition to the family of grandchildren.

Edward and Janette have both been active in their local church, serving in various capacities as Sunday-school teachers and board members.

Contents

Characters

Joshua Chadwick Jones — Josh was raised by his grand-father, great uncle and young aunt after his own parents were killed in an accident when he was only a baby. Once Josh reached his late teens, he lived with his Aunt Lou and her preacher husband, Nat Crawford, and went to school in town. On the weekends he returned to the farm to spend time with the men-folk.

Lou Jones Crawford — Though she was his aunt, Lou was only a few years older than Josh. Now Lou is a parson's wife and anxious to be a mother after losing her first child at birth.

Grandpa — The owner of the farm where Josh grew up and the only father Josh has known.

Uncle Charlie — The quiet yet supportive brother of Grandpa. For many years they have run the farm and the household together.

Willie — Josh's boyhood friend. They shared many adventures and a strong, personal commitment to their faith.

Camellia — Josh's first love, though he soon realized that his faith and her faithlessness were not compatible.

Mr. and Mrs. Foggelson — Camellia's mother and father. He was the local schoolmaster and raised concerns with his teaching of evolution. She had been a Christian until her marriage.

Chapter 1

Decisions

"Have you decided yet?"

Willie's insistent voice demanded my attention. I swiveled around to get a look at him, for the words didn't make any sense to me at all.

"What do you plan to do—after graduation?" he prodded. "Are you gonna be a minister—or what?"

Or what? my mind echoed in frustration. *What?*

I had been asking myself the same question over and over, just as Willie was asking me now. And I still didn't have an answer. Graduation was only a month away, and it seemed that I was the only one in our small town school who didn't know exactly what to do with life after the big day. It wasn't that I hadn't given it a thought. In fact, I thought about it most of the time. I prayed about it, too, and my family members kept assuring me that they were praying as well. But I still didn't have an answer to Willie's question, except to say honestly, "No—I don't know yet." And I'd been saying that for a long, long time.

I must have been frowning, and I guess Willie understood my dilemma. He didn't wait for my answer—not in words, anyway; instead he went right on talking.

"God has different timing for different people, and with a reason," he mused. "That doesn't mean that He hasn't got

13

your future planned out. When it's time—"

I quit listening for a minute, and my mind jumped to other things. Willie already had his future clearly mapped out. God had called him to be a missionary; Willie would leave for a Bible school in the Eastern United States at the end of the summer. I envied Willie, I guess. "It must be a real relief to know what God wants you to do," I muttered under my breath.

"I still can't believe it," Willie was saying when I tuned back in. "I mean, most of my life—at least what I can remember of it—I've been goin' to school, day after day. And here we are about to graduate. I just can't believe it! It doesn't seem real to me yet."

I twitched my fishing pole as if I were trying to stir up some fish. Actually I was just thinking about Willie's words. It did seem strange. We had done a great deal of talking over the years about how glad we would be to graduate and leave the old school behind, and here we were on the brink of graduation and I didn't really feel glad about it at all. In fact, I felt rather scared. I never would have dared to tell any of the fellas how I was feeling—we always crowed about the day that we'd be freed from "prison." We'd run and holler and toss our caps in the air. I knew we'd have to do it to carry on the tradition. A fella was supposed to loathe school and be more than glad to be rid of it, but at the same time I got a funny feeling down in the pit of my stomach whenever I thought about graduation.

I mulled over Willie's words and squirmed on the creek bank, pretending to have a kink in my back from sitting in one spot for so long waiting on a fish to decide he was hungry. I wiggled my pole again and noticed that I'd lost the bait off the hook. I hoped Willie didn't notice. I didn't feel much like fishing anymore and I didn't want to be bothered with baiting my hook again. Still, I wasn't ready to head for the house yet, either.

I couldn't remember much about life without school, just like Willie had said. When I was honest with myself, I knew

I'd miss the daily lessons, the recesses, the access to books. Maybe I'd miss it a whole lot, but I wasn't about to share my thoughts with anyone—not even Willie.

'Course, Willie needn't worry, I reminded myself, almost enviously. *Come fall, he'll be off to a new school, new books, and new friends.* I squirmed again.

"Here," said Willie, "lean against this stump for a while."

"Naw," I responded slowly, casting a glance at the sky. "It's almost time for chores anyway. And the fish sure aren't bitin' today."

Willie's eyes twinkled the way they did when he was trying to hold back something that made him want to laugh. I had seen the same look on his face when our teacher held his book upside down when lecturing to the class, and when Agatha Marshall took a bite of her sandwich and ate the ant that had been crawling on it, and when we tied Avery's shoelaces together as he lounged on the school grass waiting for the bell to ring.

I looked at Willie suspiciously now.

"Never seen fish bite without bait, Josh," he said, the twinkle openly showing in a grin now. "You haven't had bait on that hook for the last half hour," Willie informed me with a chuckle.

"So why didn't you tell me?" I threw at him, trying to sound miffed.

Willie sobered. "Didn't think you cared about fishin'. Your thoughts have been off someplace else all day."

I jerked up my empty hook and set about wiping it carefully on the grass and removing it from the line. Willie let me work in silence until I had finished with my fishing gear.

"You still bothered about Camellia?" he finally ventured as we picked up our gear and started down the trail to the farm.

"Camellia?" My head swung up at her name.

Willie held my eyes with a steady gaze. The question was still there, unanswered. I couldn't hide much from him, and

I sure did need someone to talk to. I decided to stop playing games.

"I guess so—a little. I mean, here we are, almost finished with school—and I've been praying and praying, and trying an' trying to show Camellia that the Bible is right, no matter what her pa says, an' she still won't even listen to a thing I have to say. She'll be done with school, too, Willie, and then she plans to move off somewhere and take some training to be a decorator—"

"Interior designer," Willie corrected.

"Interior designer," I amended with a shrug. "Who knows who she'll meet or what she'll get herself into in some god-forsaken city somewhere—"

"New York," said Willie. "Her pa says New York. If you wanta learn from the best, then you need to go to New York."

"New York? That's even worse than I thought!" I raged. "That's about as wicked a city as there is."

Willie just nodded his head solemnly.

We trudged on in silence, me wrestling with the idea of Camellia alone in a city like New York. Then Willie cut into my thoughts again.

"You still care about her, Josh?"

For some reason the question caught me wrong. Of course I cared about Camellia! She was a friend, wasn't she? And we were commanded to care about—or love—everyone, weren't we? Willie knew the Bible as well as I did. He knew I was supposed to care about Camellia.

"That's a dumb question!" I threw at Willie. "We're *supposed* to care. I've been praying for Camellia for years now— Nat and Lou have been praying, too. We all—"

"That's not what I mean, Josh, an' you know it," Willie cut in. "Do you still like Camellia?"

I wasn't prepared to answer that. In the first place I didn't see that it was any of Willie's business, even if he was my friend. In the second place, though I didn't want to think about it at the moment, I wasn't sure of the answer myself. Did I still care for Camellia—as a girl, not as just a human?

I had given up any special friendship with Camellia because she and I did not have the same spiritual values. In fact, Camellia declared that anything to do with religion was silly and superstitious. She didn't even believe that God existed, she said. Religion was a crutch for insecure people. But I believed with all my heart that God not only existed but had sent His Son to die for *me*, for my wrongdoings, and that He had a special plan for my life. How could I even consider a special relationship with Camellia? I couldn't, I knew, but I kept hoping and praying that Camellia would become a believer and then—then— Now, here we were at school's end, and still Camellia would not even listen to my side of the argument. There was more than one reason why graduation bothered me.

Willie did not pursue the question.

"Are you coming to town for the social tomorrow night?" he asked.

It was a church social—one of the few activities meant just for our age group, and they were always fun. Aunt Lou and Uncle Nat saw to that. Several teenagers from town had started coming to church as a result of the socials that Uncle Nat organized. Most of the young people eagerly anticipated the monthly social, and I enjoyed them, too. At any other time I would have answered Willie with an enthusiastic, "Sure, I'll be there," but instead I mumbled, "I'll see."

"Well, sure hope you can make it." Willie shifted his pole and the one fish he had caught into his left hand so he'd have his right one free to untie his horse from the hitching rail.

I hadn't been very good company, and suddenly I felt ashamed because of it. It wasn't Willie's fault that Camellia still wasn't a believer, and it wasn't Willie's fault that I still didn't know what God wanted me to do with my life, and it wasn't Willie's fault that graduation was quickly approaching with its unsettled questions. Willie had no more control of the ticking clock than I did. I had no right to be owly and disagreeable with Willie.

I tried hard to shift my troubled thoughts to the back of

my mind and bid my friend the kind of goodbye he deserved.

"Thanks, Willie," I said, and then didn't quite know how to finish. "Thanks for coming out."

I saw the twinkle in Willie's eye again.

"Sorry the fish weren't biting."

"Next time I might even try using a little bait," I teased back. "Though at least now I don't have fish to clean and can loaf a bit before chorin'."

Willie looked down at the one fish that dangled beside his saddle. A mock frown crossed his face.

"I think I might just stop off and present a fish to Mary Turley," he said, "and invite her to the social tomorrow night." I wasn't sure if Willie was serious or not.

We both laughed and Willie moved his horse off down the lane.

"See you tomorrow night, Josh," he called back to me.

I answered as he knew I would. "I'll be there."

Chapter 2

The Social

That next night I hurried through my chores and ran for my bedroom to bathe and change. After adjusting my tie and slicking down my hair, I picked up my jacket and started down the stairs, avoiding the step with the worst creak.

"Big night tonight, Boy?"

The question came from Grandpa. He and Uncle Charlie were sitting at the kitchen table going over some farm bills together.

I grinned. I guess the night was no bigger than any other social night, but it still was pretty special to me. I nodded.

"Nat says the Youth Group is really growin'," continued Grandpa.

I nodded again, then added, " 'Bout twenty of us now."

"That's good," said Grandpa. "Any of the new ones comin' to church too?"

"Yeah, three of 'em are."

"Good!" said Grandpa again.

Uncle Charlie took a gulp of coffee and let the legs of his chair hit the worn kitchen linoleum with a dull thud. He looked me over carefully, from the crease in my best pants to the straight part of my hair. Then he nodded, as though I passed inspection.

19

"Enjoy youth, Joshua," Grandpa said. "The cares of adulthood will be upon ya soon enough."

I couldn't help but smile. Grandpa knew little about *youth*. If he thought that I wouldn't have any worries or concerns until I stepped out into the adult world, he was all wrong. Or he had forgotten. He had no idea about the things I had been grappling with lately. But I let it pass as though the only thought in my mind was a night of games and singing, followed by some of Lou's punch and cake. But at Grandpa's words I could feel my mood change somewhat. I wasn't in quite the same hurry that I had been a few minutes before.

Uncle Charlie's sharp eyes were on me again. He was searching for something, I knew. I mustered a grin and moved out of his range. I didn't want to be answering any questions. Not that Uncle Charlie would ask—not outright, anyway—but I felt the probing and had always squirmed some under it.

"I shouldn't be too late," I said as a parting remark of some kind. They knew I'd come straight home as soon as the social was over, and that it would be well chaperoned by Uncle Nat and Aunt Lou.

"Take yer time. Have fun," Grandpa responded.

The thought of Aunt Lou filled me with a bit of concern. Her baby was due in a couple of weeks, and after what had happened with her first baby I was uneasy about her. Over and over she assured me that there was no need to worry. She had lost little Amanda because she had had the measles during the pregnancy. Aunt Lou had been the picture of health all through this one. Doc had told her over and over that the baby seemed healthy and energetic. He was predicting a strong baby boy, but Aunt Lou still had her heart set on another daughter, and I guess I secretly hoped for a girl, too.

In the barn I was greeted by Chester, the beautiful bay that Grandpa and Uncle Charlie had surprised me with on my last birthday. I still couldn't believe that such a horse was really mine. I patted his shining round rump and reached for the saddle. He nickered at me and rubbed his nose against my chest looking for a treat from my pocket.

"Cut that out," I scolded him. "You'll mess my Sunday clothes!" But he didn't care about that; he went right on sniffing and blowing. I moved so he couldn't reach me and smoothed the blanket for the saddle.

I walked Chester out of the barn, closed the door securely, and mounted. Chester was eager to be on the road, even if I had forgotten to bring him his sugar lump or bit of apple. I had to rein him in to keep him from leaving the farmyard on a dead run. Grandpa didn't take too kindly to running animals, but it sure was tempting when I was up on Chester. He loved to run, and his strong legs and smooth body fairly trembled with excitement whenever he was turned toward the road.

It was a warm spring night. The sun was still lighting my way, but I knew that by the time I returned home it would be dark. Chester could find his way back to his stall in total darkness if need be, but it would be nicer traveling by moonlight. Only a few carelessly drifting clouds crossed the sky; the moon should give some light later on.

My thoughts turned back to the social, and I wondered if there would be any new young people there. Wouldn't it be something if Camellia decided to come! *Maybe if more of the girls her age . . .* I thought. But there were several girls Camellia's age who attended, and that had never influenced her before. Nothing, in fact, seemed to influence Camellia in favor of coming to church.

As I began going over the list of who might be in attendance, my eagerness to get there increased. Chester must have sensed my feelings, for before I knew it we were racing down the dusty road at a reckless pace. I reined Chester in, and he snorted in disgust. He tossed his head and pranced along the roadway, fighting against the bit while I busied myself trying to brush the dust from my dress clothes.

In spite of my intentions to be there early, young people were already milling about when I entered the churchyard. I tied Chester securely and called out hellos as I hurried to the parsonage to see if I could help Aunt Lou with any last-minute preparations.

"Josh!" she called out excitedly. "Good to see you! How are things at the farm?"

Aunt Lou always greeted me as though we hadn't seen one another for months, when the fact was that I had left town to stay at the farm only the day before.

"Fine," I responded. "Just fine. How are you?"

Aunt Lou looked down at her expanding front. She placed a hand tenderly on the growing baby and smiled at me.

"We are both just fine, aren't we, honey?" she said to her unborn child.

I smiled. Aunt Lou talked to her baby all the time. I was used to it by now. And she did look fine—her eyes shone and her cheeks glowed.

"Is there anything I can do to help?" I asked.

"Everything is already done. Nat is over at the church and we carried all of the refreshments over earlier."

"I'm sorry I was so late—" I began, but Aunt Lou stopped me.

"You're not late. Everyone else is just early. Impatient to get started, I guess. My, how this group has grown! I hardly know how much food to fix anymore."

I could tell by the smile on Aunt Lou's face that she was pleased to have such a problem.

We walked the short distance across the churchyard together. Other young people were arriving, calling excitedly back and forth.

I was lounging on the outside steps talking to some of the fellas when a rig rounded the corner and headed our way. At first I thought it must be someone new, and then I recognized Willie. Willie never drove; he always rode horseback, same as me. It *was* Willie, all right—and he wasn't alone, either.

For a moment none of us spoke. We just stood there gawking as Willie climbed down and tied the horse, and then reached a hand up to help a girl step down. She was wearing a full-skirted pink dress and she had her hair piled up on her head with little curls spilling down here and there. She looked familiar, yet I couldn't place her. Willie had tied his horse some distance away from the steps where we waited. We all stood there, straining to figure out who Willie was with.

"By jingo!" hissed Tom Newton, "it's Mary Turley—an' all dolled up, too."

It can't be, I thought. *Surely he wasn't serious!* But, sure enough, there was ol' Willie leading Mary Turley up the walkway to the church.

I wanted to laugh, to howl at Willie. My first impulse was to slap him on the back and tease him some, but I didn't. I stood there quietly and watched.

Mary had certainly changed! And so had Willie—he was so spiffed up and shining I scarcely knew him. And he seemed so gentlemanly and grown-up too. All of us were put to silence by it all, and I bet other fellas besides me were wondering why we hadn't thought of inviting Mary ourselves.

Mary smiled shyly at us as she brushed by, and Willie gave me just the slightest wink. I was sure no one else had seen it, but I caught it, just as I caught that twinkle in his eye.

Avery gave me a hard jab in the ribs that made me gasp for air, and then we all shuffled and moved on the steps and made an about-face as we followed Willie and Mary into the church.

We found some places to sit. As usual, the girls sorta lined up in the seats on the south side of the building and the fellas took the seats on the north. All except Willie, that is. He seated Mary alongside Martha Ingrim, but instead of coming over to the boys, he sat down right beside her!

Uncle Nat took charge of the meeting, calling it to order by welcoming everyone and having first-timers introduced. There was another new girl from town too, but she had come with Thelma and Virginia Brown, so none of us paid much attention.

Then Willie introduced Mary. He spoke clearly and without embarrassment. I couldn't help but marvel at the way he handled it.

"This is Mary Turley," he said. "Mary lives out our way. We—Josh and I, and several others here—went to school with Mary for a number of years."

As we played some games, there was some mixing up of the seating, and Willie and Mary got separated. But Mary seemed to be having a good time. I was glad to see that she felt at home among us.

I had always thought of Mary as a plain girl, and maybe she really was, but tonight she was pretty in her own way. She had a smile that drew smiles in return, and her eyes were deep and intense. Her manner kept my eyes wandering back to her. She seemed so grown-up and self-assured compared to most of the girls I knew.

And then I remembered why I hadn't seen much of Mary for the last several years. Her ma had been sick, and Mary had needed to take over the running of the household and the cooking of the meals. She hadn't been able to go on to school in town like she had wanted to. I hadn't given it much thought when I heard about it. But now, looking at Mary, I realized she had likely done more growing up than the rest of us who hadn't borne similar responsibilities.

Not at all somber or morose, she laughed and enjoyed the games as much as anyone at the social, but she did carry the air of one who had learned a good measure of self-assurance.

After the games were over, Uncle Nat brought out his guitar and we gathered in a circle and sang every hymn we knew by heart. Mary didn't seem to know many of the words, but she listened in appreciation and once or twice I noticed her small foot tapping in time with the music. Though I wasn't sitting close enough to her to be sure, I had the feeling that she was humming right along.

When Aunt Lou served refreshments, Mary volunteered her help. I was busy pouring the punch, so we exchanged a few pleasantries. I asked about her ma, feeling apologetic that I hadn't taken more of an interest sooner. Mary smiled when she told me that her ma was much better—even able to be back in her own kitchen again.

I thought of Mrs. Turley and that big kitchen. I well remembered the day that Willie, Avery, and I stopped by on the way back from our hike along the creek. We were half-starved, and Mrs. Turley's well-stocked kitchen had about saved our lives. I remembered Mary too, a rather gangly, freckle-faced girl at the time. I never would have dreamed that she would become the well-poised young lady that I saw before me now.

"I'm glad about your ma," I assured her.

"Me, too," said Mary. "It was hard to see her so sick."

There was no mention about the hard years that she had put in being housekeeper and nursemaid. She just seemed to have a sincere appreciation that her ma was feeling better.

"Maybe you can come to our next social," I dared venture.

"I'd love to," responded Mary and I could tell by her shining eyes that she really meant it. I wanted Mary to be a part of our Youth Group. I wanted her to feel welcome. Yet she really wasn't a believer, and I couldn't help but question Willie's actions. Here he was courting a girl who was not a Christian, and I—I had to give up my relationship with Camellia for that very reason. It didn't seem fair somehow, and yet I had no doubts about Willie and his commitment to his faith. Still—was Willie taking chances going out with a non-Christian girl? My line of reasoning directed my thoughts to Camellia and they lingered there, remembering her sparkling eyes, her long, burnished tresses. She was the prettiest girl I had ever seen. *If only*—but my thoughts were interrupted by Aunt Lou's call for me to refill the punch glasses.

Chapter 3

Great News

All the next week we had glorious spring weather, and folks began talking about spring fever. I don't know exactly what kind of fever hit me, but I had an awful time concentrating on my studies.

Final exams were just a few weeks away, and our grades on those finals could have a great deal to do with our being accepted into college. Maybe that was why I was having such a difficult time. Most of the others already had a college picked and a vocation to pursue as well. Daily, it seemed, someone asked me, "What are your plans, Josh?" and I would mumble, red-faced, that I still hadn't decided for sure.

For sure? That made it sound like I had several considerations. The truth was, I was about as far from knowing what the future held for me as I had been on the first day I climbed the steps of the schoolhouse.

I avoided folks as much as I could. I didn't want to answer any questions when I still didn't really have an answer.

As a result, I hung around home a lot. I pretended to be studying, and Aunt Lou and Uncle Nat certainly approved of that. I was trying, but my mind just didn't seem to want to stay with the books.

On one particularly lovely spring evening, when the fragrant smell of early spring blossoms wafted in my open window, making it even more difficult to concentrate, I sat at my small desk trying hard to think through the math computations before me, but my mind refused to deal with the equations.

My thoughts insisted on flitting about. Graduation was getting nearer with each passing day. I thought of my future still unplanned, as far as I could see. I thought of Camellia and her intention to leave for distant New York and her training in Interior Design. How would she ever manage in such a big, indifferent city? How could her father sanction such a venture?

The soft spring breeze brought a fresh whisper of fragrance to my nose and reminded me of the roses along the creek bank every springtime. I could picture the young blades of greenery poking their slim heads through the soil. I could almost smell the freshness of the gently flowing water and hear the splash of a fish breaking the surface to snatch at a fly, then slip back into the coolness of the stream again.

The call of the creek turned my thoughts to Gramps. I still hadn't gotten used to his being gone. Each time that I went home to the farm I found myself searching for signs of him. The empty chair at the table looked too forlorn, the place where his worn farm sweater had hung looked bare and dejected, the padded chair by the well-lit kitchen window where he sat to read his Bible and work his crossword puzzles looked far too lonely.

I wouldn't have wished him back; I knew that. He had gone to a far better place than his dwelling here had been. But even that thought did not erase the ache I carried around with me.

Even though I stayed here in town during the week with Aunt Lou and Uncle Nat, I loved the farm. I loved the soil. I treasured the spot that held my roots buried so deeply. I loved the springtime and the planting of the seeds. I loved the summer as we watched the green begin to appear and then mature as the weeks passed by. I loved the autumn, when it was so evident that God was good and was again supplying the needs of His people.

Even the winter months were enjoyable. I loved the frosty mornings when the steam rose from the pail of warm milk I carried from the barn to the house. I loved the smell of the warm straw I spread out to bed down Bossie or one of her stallmates. I loved the soft mewing of the barn cats as they coaxed for their morning breakfast of warm, fresh milk.

The farm was a good place to be. I guess I loved most everything about it.

And then I thought again of Grandpa and Uncle Charlie, and suddenly a new thought occurred to me. What would happen to the farm when they were no longer able to care for it? I had never thought about it before; I just assumed that they would always be there, farming, just like they had been doing ever since I could recollect. But of course they wouldn't. Couldn't. The quickly passing years were taking their toll on Grandpa and Uncle Charlie. They didn't walk as erectly or as quickly as they used to. Even I could see that. And Uncle Charlie seemed to be faring a bit worse than Grandpa. I had noticed it the last time we had chored together. He was getting much slower in movement than he used to be, even a bit clumsy with his hands. I'd had to undo the knot that tied the gunny sack of grain. He had tried but couldn't manage it.

The thought of Uncle Charlie and Grandpa no longer able to carry on the farming made me restless and uneasy. I couldn't imagine life without the farm. It didn't matter if God called me to be a preacher in some far-off city or even a missionary, like Willie, to some distant land, I still wanted to think of the farm as home. I still wanted to be able to visit it when I had opportunity, to bring my family, if I ever had one, to feel the kinship with the soil and to watch things grow. I felt that my roots would always be there in that land that Grandpa had tilled ever since I could remember. To sever those roots would in some way be losing a part of me.

My reverie was interrupted by a soft whine under my feet.

"Pixie!" I said. "I didn't know you were here. I haven't been paying much attention to you, have I, girl?" The little dog wagged her tail happily and jumped into my lap. I snapped shut my math book and pushed it aside. I couldn't study now. I needed a break. Pixie jumped down as I stood and stretched. "Maybe I'll go to the kitchen for some of Aunt Lou's cookies and a glass of milk." I was about to leave the room when I sensed more than I actually heard a strange commotion in the kitchen.

It wasn't loud and it wasn't hasty. It was just different somehow. I listened more carefully; for a time I heard nothing. Pixie ran to the door and barked softly; then I heard the quick, quiet step of Uncle Nat approaching my door. I stood motionless, my hand going up to push back the hair that flopped over my forehead.

Uncle Nat didn't even knock. He opened the door gently and poked in his head. He was wearing his hat, something that Uncle Nat didn't usually do in the house.

"Lou says it's time, Josh," he said in almost a whisper. "I'm going for Doc."

My mouth went dry and my breath seemed to catch in my chest. *It was time.* The very thought sent a shiver of fear running all through me. I had known all along that we would face this eventually, yet I still wasn't prepared.

For some reason the little unknown somebody that Aunt Lou had been carrying had seemed so safe and protected as long as her body enclosed it. But now it was time for this baby to enter the world—a world where sickness and dangers abounded. Would the little one make it? To face the loss of another baby would be too much for any of us to bear.

I wanted to run to Aunt Lou to assure myself that she was all right, but my feet refused to move. I tried swallowing, but my mouth was too dry. I felt like urging Uncle Nat to hurry, but I realized we had things rather backward.

"I'll run for Doc," I managed to say. "You stay with Aunt Lou."

Uncle Nat didn't argue. He stepped wordlessly aside so I could leave the room.

I was almost to the kitchen door before he called softly after me, "No need to run, Josh. Lou says there is lots of time."

I heard him, but I was already running by the time I had reached the back door. By the time I left the parsonage yard I was in full stride.

All the way to Doc's house I prayed urgently for Aunt Lou. I prayed for the new baby. I prayed that Doc wouldn't be out in the country somewhere on a house call.

By the time I reached Doc's front door I was breathing hard. I rapped loudly and stepped back to wait. I could hear movement inside, and that was encouraging. Doc answered the door himself and didn't even make a comment when he saw me standing there, my sides heaving from running. He just reached to the hat tree by the door to retrieve his hat and picked up his black bag from the small table, all in one motion, and called out to his wife that he would be at the parsonage, and we were gone.

We didn't run. Doc's slower pace frustrated me, and I found it hard to match his methodical stride, but I did try. We walked in silence until Doc seemed to feel I had enough breath to talk.

"When did the contractions start?" he asked me.

"I dunno," I admitted dumbly. "Uncle Nat just came to my room and said it's time."

"Did Lou have supper with you?" Doc asked further.

"She—she—" I thought back. "She was at table with us, but she didn't eat much. Just sorta pushed her food around on her plate."

I hadn't paid much attention to it at the time.

"She didn't say anything," I added.

"She wouldn't," commented Doc, and he picked up speed, for which I was thankful.

When we reached the house Uncle Nat was not there to greet us. Doc knew the way to the bedroom, so after letting him in, I knew there was little else that I could do—except keep praying.

The time dragged on forever. Or so it seemed. In reality I guess that things happened in good time and order. But for me, it seemed an eternity. I paced back and forth in the kitchen, and I paced back and forth on the porch, and I paced back and forth on the front board walk that led up to the small parsonage.

At last I heard the small, funny, squeaky cry of a newborn, and I knew it was finally over. I strained with my whole body to catch any further sounds. I guess I was listening for a cry from Aunt Lou. None came. And then I heard laughter and the voice of Uncle Nat raised in prayerful thanksgiving. I breathed again and ran toward the back entrance.

Uncle Nat met me in the kitchen, his face beaming. We didn't even speak to one another, just stopped long enough for a quick embrace and then hurried on to the bedroom. I suppose there were tears on both our cheeks, tears of relief and joy.

Doc was talking when I entered the room. I wasn't sure if he was talking to Aunt Lou or the tiny bundle he held in his big hands.

"Sure surprised me," he was saying. "I was looking for a big, bouncing boy, but just look at this young'un. Healthy and hearty as you please."

Lou was smiling a contented, love-filled smile. She still looked pale to me—but, oh, did she look happy!

Doc continued speaking to Aunt Lou. "You did a fine job, little lady—and just look at your reward. Beautiful baby. Just beautiful. Reminds me of her mamma when I delivered her some twenty-odd years ago."

The word *her* caught my attention. It was a girl! Aunt Lou's dream had come true and Doc's "big boy" had been a girl instead. I grinned and suddenly felt shy and awkward. I hung back a bit, not really knowing what to do or say. Aunt Lou sensed it immediately. She raised slightly from her pillows and held out her hand to me.

"Come see her, Josh," she encouraged. "Like Doc says, she's beautiful."

I moved slowly forward just as Doc reached down and laid the precious bundle in Aunt Lou's arms. The little face was red and wrinkled and her eyes were almost squinted shut. She had a thatch of dark hair that for the moment was plastered tightly to the well-shaped little head. She really wasn't all that beautiful, as Doc and Aunt Lou were insisting, but even I knew she was very special.

And then she waved a small fist frantically in the air and went searching for it with a puckered-up mouth. Miraculously, she managed to connect the two and began sucking noisily. We all laughed and Aunt Lou held her even closer and Uncle Nat's eyes filled with tears again. She *was* beautiful.

When Aunt Lou could speak again she looked down at her baby and then up at me. "Sarah Jane," she said, "meet your cousin, Joshua Jones. He's about the finest cousin a little girl could ever have. You're a lucky little girl, Sarah Jane— No, not lucky—blessed." Aunt Lou gave me one of her special smiles. I could feel the firm arm of Uncle Nat about my shoulders, and it gave me a warm, family feeling.

I looked down again at the tiny bundle in Aunt Lou's arms. Since my own folks had died, Aunt Lou had been like a mother and aunt all rolled up in one. Now I had little Sarah Jane too. I might not be all that Aunt Lou had generously boasted me to be, but I knew one thing. I loved that little bundle with all of my being, and I knew instinctively that no harm would ever come to her that I had the power to stop.

Chapter 4

Sharing the News

"Somebody's gotta go to the farm!" I burst out excitedly, tearing my eyes from the baby and Aunt Lou to implore Uncle Nat.

"I guess that can wait 'til morning," Uncle Nat said, and I could see he wasn't too anxious to leave his wife and new daughter.

"Morning? This news will never keep until morning. And Grandpa and Uncle Charlie would never forgive us!"

"It's pretty late," Uncle Nat continued. He reached down to lift his pocket watch. "It's almost midnight." Then he spoke to brand-new little Sarah Jane. "You missed being born on your grandmother's birthday by about ten minutes, little one."

Uncle Nat didn't talk about his ma too often, but I could tell by his tone that he would have been real pleased if Sarah had prolonged her coming just a bit.

I wasn't put off by Uncle Nat's diversion.

"Midnight or not," I went on, "someone should go out to the farm. I can go. Chester could find his way even if it was pitch dark—and it's not. Looks really light out yet. Moon must be shining—"

"Well, Lou?" Uncle Nat asked. Lou just smiled and nodded. "Bring me a pen and the writing tablet," she said, and

I knew it was decided that I could go.

Aunt Lou had to have her hands free to write, so Uncle Nat lifted the small bundle of baby from her arms and began pacing the floor with her, talking softly to her all the while. I didn't listen to what he said, but now and then I caught a word. He was already telling her about God. Imagine! A tiny tyke like that, and Uncle Nat was already preaching the little one her first sermon.

Aunt Lou found it a bit difficult to write, propped up on her pillows like she was. I guess she wanted to tell Grandpa and Uncle Charlie about the new baby herself, because she seemed to write on and on. I wondered how she could find so much to say about someone she had just met, so to speak.

At last she was done and folded that paper and handed it to me and laid the tablet and the pen on the small night table by her bed. She smiled again—that contented, happy smile—but I could see she was really tired.

A movement caused us all to look at the doorway. It was Doc. I had quite forgotten about him. Guess he had been in the kitchen having himself a cup of tea while we all got acquainted with Sarah Jane, and now he was back again to check everything one more time and tuck Aunt Lou and the baby in for the night. I kissed Aunt Lou on the cheek, took one more look at Sarah Jane to see if she had grown or changed any yet. I was always hearing ladies exclaim how quickly babies did that. But she looked just the same to me, only she had fallen asleep—right in the middle of Uncle Nat's sermon.

Chester seemed to sense my mood, and once we were on the road he was ready to run. I guess he thought that this time he might be able to get away with it. I didn't let him though, for even though there was a bit of a moon and even though his night-eyes were better than mine, I still knew it was unwise to let a horse travel at full gallop in the dark.

It seemed to take an especially long time to cover the distance to the farm. Normally I would let my mind wander to many things, but tonight I could only think of the new baby. Whole and well and brand new and Doc said that she was fine, just fine.

At last I reached the farm and was a bit surprised to see the house all dark. But I should have known it would be. Grandpa and Uncle Charlie went to bed somewhere around ten each night, and this night being no different than any other as far as they were concerned, they would have followed their usual pattern.

I argued briefly with myself as to whether to flip Chester's rein over the gate post and run in with the news or to take Chester to the barn—as would need to be done eventually anyway—and then go to the house. I decided to go ahead and bed Chester down. It was hard to make myself go to the barn first but I knew I would hate to come back out to care for Chester after I had delivered the good news.

Chester was glad to see his own stall. I didn't figure him to be too hungry, knowing that he had already been well fed, but I hurriedly forked him a bit of hay just in case he had a notion to eat. He started in on it right away.

I scarcely took the time to secure the barn door before I was off to the house on the run. It was a fair distance between the house and the barn—a fact I had never particularly noted before. I was puffing by the time I hit the back porch. The back door, as usual, was not locked. I wasn't sure my Grandpa could lock it even if he wanted to. I pushed it open and it squeaked just a bit.

I wanted to holler out my news, but my good sense held me in check. If I came in shouting I'd scare Grandpa and Uncle Charlie half to death.

I climbed the steps quickly, trying not to make too much noise. I never even thought about the squeaky one until I heard it protest beneath my foot.

"Who is it?" Grandpa called out.

"Me," I answered in a whispery voice.

I heard Uncle Charlie stirring, but the noise didn't come from his bed. He was sitting near his window in the old chair. I knew then that he had watched me ride into the yard, take

Chester to the barn and run for the house.

For a moment I forgot about Grandpa, about Aunt Lou, even about the new baby.

"What are you doing up?" I quizzed Uncle Charlie.

"Nothin' much," he answered evasively. "Just can't git along with my bed sometimes."

Grandpa called out again, "Be right there." I could hear the bed springs groaning as he lifted himself from the bed and began to pull on his pants.

"I take it you have some news," Grandpa said as he came out of the bedroom, a lighted lamp in his hand.

"Sure do," I beamed, my thoughts jumping immediately back to Sarah Jane.

"Well?" prompted Uncle Charlie.

"Another girl," I fairly cheered. "And she is just fine."

"And Lou?" asked Grandpa. In his heart he knew very well that I wouldn't be grinning from ear to ear unless Aunt Lou was just fine, too. But Lou was his little girl, and Grandpa wouldn't be at ease until he heard it said.

"Fine!" I said. "Just fine—an' happy."

"Thank you, Father!" Grandpa said softly and I understood his little prayer of gratitude. Then he began to grin. I could see his face by the light of the lamp he held in his hand. He was beaming.

Uncle Charlie had moved to join us in the hallway. He was grinning too—a wide, infectious smile. He looked about the happiest I had ever seen him. But I was surprised at how slowly he moved. Grandpa turned to him with concern in his eyes and voice.

"Another bad night?" he asked, and Uncle Charlie nodded. I didn't understand the question—or the answer. Why was Uncle Charlie having bad nights? Why was he moving toward the stairs like an old man? Why did he reach out a hand to assist himself as he descended? I hadn't known about any of this. Why hadn't someone informed me?

"Was Doc there?" Uncle Charlie asked. He knew that

sometimes Doc was out on one call when he was needed elsewhere.

"Got him myself," I explained. "He was right at home when I went for him."

"Was Nat there?" asked Grandpa, and I knew that Grandpa was thinking of the last time.

"All the time," I answered.

"Good!" said Grandpa, and he beamed some more as he set the lamp on the kitchen table.

Uncle Charlie shuffled to the stove, shook it up, and put in a few more sticks of wood. The stove had been banked for the night; before long the wood caught and I could hear the blaze grow. Uncle Charlie pushed forward the coffeepot.

"Tell us about her," Grandpa was saying, excitement filling his voice.

Uncle Charlie eased a chair toward the table and lowered himself slowly onto it. He leaned forward eagerly, not wanting to miss a word.

"She's not very big," I started, indicating with my hands, much as I often did when I told a fish story.

" 'Course not," cut in Grandpa.

"An' she—she—" How could I say that she was red and wrinkled and sort of puffy? Would they understand?

"Has she any hair?"

"Lots of it—dark."

"Just like Lou," cut in Grandpa.

"What color are her eyes?" Uncle Charlie asked.

"I—I—don't really know. She didn't open them much, but they are sorta dark, I guess."

"Did Doc say how much she weighs?"

I hadn't heard him say anything about her weight. I just shook my head.

"Tell us about Lou," Grandpa was prompting.

"Well—"

"Was it a long—?" began Grandpa again.

It had seemed half of forever to me, but I shrugged and said honestly, "Doc said it was real good. Real good. I went for him about quarter-to-nine and Sarah was born just before midnight."

Grandpa and Uncle Charlie exchanged grins and nods and I understood that they were well satisfied with that.

"But Aunt Lou says that she was having some—some—"

"Contractions."

"Yeah, from about one o'clock on. But they didn't get strong until about suppertime." I didn't want them to get the idea that it had been too easy.

"But she's fine now?" This was from Grandpa again.

"Just fine," I reassured him.

Uncle Charlie eased himself off his chair and went for the coffeepot. I wasn't sure that the coffee would be hot enough yet, but perhaps Uncle Charlie needed something to occupy his hands.

He poured three cups and brought two of them, a bit of steam rising from each, to the table. He passed one cup to Grandpa and put one down in front of me. It was the first time I noticed that his fingers looked funny. I was about to ask if he had hurt his hand when I noticed that the other hand looked the same way. I shut my mouth quickly on the unasked question and looked at Grandpa, but he didn't seem to read the question in my eyes. I guess he was still too busy celebrating his new granddaughter.

"Her name," he said suddenly. "You haven't told us her name."

"It's Sarah," I told him. "Sarah Jane."

"That's nice," said Grandpa, and Uncle Charlie, who was just returning to the table with his own cup of coffee, repeated the name after me. "Sarah Jane," he said, "Sarah Jane. That's nice."

I suddenly remembered Aunt Lou's letter. I fished it from my pocket and handed it to Grandpa. He opened it eagerly and began to read it aloud to Uncle Charlie. There wasn't much more for me to say about little Sarah Jane. Aunt Lou was saying it all.

We sat and drank our coffee and chatted some more about

the new baby and Aunt Lou and Uncle Nat. But watching Uncle Charlie's clumsy fingers try to lift the coffee cup to his mouth took some of the joy out of the event for me. He spilled a bit as he tried to drink. I noticed the dark liquid dribble over his fingers more than once as he raised the cup to his mouth. Maybe this was why Uncle Charlie didn't let the coffee get as steaming hot as he used to.

I thought of all the times I had watched Uncle Charlie lift the cup to his lips and take a full gulp of steaming hot coffee and somehow manage to swallow it with no harm done. But he had steady hands then. Not gnarled fingers that couldn't grip things tightly.

"I'm pretty tired I guess," I finally excused myself. "Think I'll go on up to bed."

Grandpa was still grinning but he stifled a yawn. "Me, too," he said and reached for the lamp.

"You two go ahead," Uncle Charlie waved us on. "I think I'll just sit here for a bit longer. Maybe have another cup."

I looked at Grandpa.

"Did you take one of the pills?" he asked.

Uncle Charlie nodded.

"Still no relief?"

"Some." Both Grandpa and I knew that Uncle Charlie wasn't admitting to much.

Grandpa left the lamp on the table and we climbed the stairs without it.

When we got up to the hallway I reached out a hand to Grandpa.

"What is it?" I asked in a whisper.

Grandpa didn't seem to understand my question.

"What's the matter with Uncle Charlie?" I asked then.

"What do you mean?"

"His hands—all—all twisted, and his walk so slow and—"

"Oh, that," responded Grandpa matter-of-factly. "That's just his arthritis. It's gettin' worse."

Arthritis! Worse! How come I'd never noticed it before?

"How long—how long has he been this way?" I found myself asking.

"He's had arthritis some for years," Grandpa responded. "But he has his good days and his bad days. Folks say the weather. It's steadily getting worse, though. It's really into his hands bad now. Used to just be in his knees and his back."

There wasn't much that I could say, so I let Grandpa go. "See you in the morning," I muttered and turned to my bedroom.

I lay awake a long time that night—thinking of more than our new Sarah Jane. I thought a great deal about Uncle Charlie. It scared me, this arthritis. Already it had made him into an old man. It had happened so gradually that I had missed it.

But not now. Now it was very obvious. Uncle Charlie was not a complainer, but it was easy to see that even small tasks were hard for him to accomplish. And how could he ever farm?

I fought for sleep, both to escape my uneasy thoughts and because I knew I would need it. Grandpa had said that we would leave for town just as soon as we could finish up the chores the next morning, and I knew without asking that Grandpa would start those chores a little earlier than usual.

Even so, it was a long time until I could lay aside my excitement—and my worry—and let sleep claim me.

Chapter 5

Graduation

It took several days for things to fall back into a normal routine. Grandpa and Uncle Charlie visited the parsonage with far more frequency than usual. I think they were a little afraid that young Sarah Jane might grow up when they weren't looking. Anyway, they came in often to check on her.

Sarah Jane greatly changed the procedures of the household. Aunt Lou didn't seem to get as much baking done as she used to, and both Uncle Nat and I found ourselves helping around the house more. That baby was either hungry or wet every five minutes.

She was a good little tyke, though. Lou kept telling Uncle Nat and me over and over what a good baby she was, and I was quite willing to take Aunt Lou's word for it. She certainly did a great deal of sleeping. Whenever I brought one of my friends in for a peek at her she was either sleeping or eating, it seemed to me, and neither one worked too well for showing her off.

She very quickly lost her redness and her wrinkles, and soon she had a soft, pinkish look and a little round head capped with dark downy hair. She opened her eyes more, too; often she would lie in my arms and look at my face as if she knew just who I was and how I fit into her life. I loved it when she looked at me that way; if no one was close enough to hear, I'd talk to her and tell her things about myself so that she really would know me. We all adored her—after all, we all loved Lou, and had waited for this special baby for a long time.

I expected that now it would be even harder to study, and in some ways it was. But suddenly it became very important for me to get good grades as I left the school system and went out into the world. I wouldn't have admitted it to a soul, but I didn't want Sarah to ever have reason to be ashamed of me. So I pitched into those textbooks like I'd never done in my whole life—and it worked, too. I ended up with the best set of marks I had ever gotten.

Willie dropped by now and then. Sometimes we studied together, and we played with Sarah, but mostly we just took a break from our books and talked. One Thursday afternoon he tapped on my window, and I could tell just by looking that he was really excited about something. I pushed back my Advanced Speller and opened the window.

"Is Sarah sleepin'?" Willie asked.

I nodded.

"Then come out." Willie didn't want to take any chances on his excitement waking the baby.

I eased the window back down quietly and headed for the back door.

"What is it?" I asked as soon as I was clear of the kitchen.

"Mary," beamed Willie. "She became a Christian."

Now I knew why Willie was excited. I was excited, too. We gave each other a big hug, pounding one another on the back. Mary had been coming to church every Sunday since she had been to the Youth Group with Willie.

"When?" I asked when I could speak.

"Just this afternoon. I came to tell you just as soon as I could."

I slapped Willie on the back again. I couldn't help but think how happy I would feel if I had the same good news about Camellia.

"That's great!" I said. "Just great."

Afraid that my tears might show, I pulled away and headed for the backyard swing that Uncle Charlie had built for Lou. Willie followed me without a word; I guess he knew I was feeling rather emotional.

Avoiding Willie's eyes, I gave a little push with one foot to start the swing in gentle motion and looked at it carefully like I had never done in the past. Uncle Charlie was skilled with simple tools. Each board was carefully fashioned and properly joined. The arm where my hand rested was polished smooth and shaped for comfort. I ran my hand idly over it, wondering if Uncle Charlie would ever be able to hold a hammer or a plane again. Then my thoughts jerked back to the present.

"What do her folks think?" I asked Willie.

"I don't know about her pa. He hasn't said much. But her ma says that it's Mary's decision and that she'll support her in her new faith. I think she wishes that she had the courage to make the commitment herself. She must have done a great deal of thinking when she was so ill."

"I suppose," I agreed.

"Mary is already praying for her ma. She says it's just a matter of time, she knows, until her ma will become a Christian too. She says she thinks that her ma has been searching for God for a long time, just hasn't known where or how to find Him. An' now that Mary knows, she can help her ma."

The excitement had grown in Willie's voice again. His eyes were shining.

"Josh," he said, "this is the first person that I have talked to about my faith, the first one to become a Christian because of it. It's—it's—well, it is the most exciting thing that has ever happened to me."

I had never had the experience myself, although I had tried—with Camellia, with her ma, even with Jack Berry in prison by letter after I finally forgave him. None of those had worked. I still prayed for all of them, though.

"Does Mary feel called to the mission field too?" I asked.

Willie looked just a bit puzzled.

"I dunno," he answered.

"Isn't that—isn't that pretty important?"

"Well, she needs to learn a bit more about being a Christian before she thinks about where God wants her, don't you think?"

"But you already know where God wants you," I pressed.

"So?" said Willie with a shrug.

"So it just might be important where He wants your girl."

"My girl?" Willie really seemed confused now.

"Mary!" I said impatiently to jog his failing memory. "The girl you just brought to the faith. Mary! If you are going to train to be a missionary, then perhaps it would be a bit handy if your girl would be one, too."

Willie looked dumbfounded.

"Mary isn't *my* girl," he said at last.

"What?"

"Where'd you ever get that idea?"

"From you," I said. "You brought her to Youth Group and you've been bringing her to church an' you—"

"But she's not my *girl*."

"Does Mary know that?" I threw back at Willie.

"Of course! We're just friends. Mary's understood that all along. We talked it over the first night I asked her to Youth Group."

"And you came together as *friends*?" It seemed preposterous to me. "You mean you brought her and talked to her and shared your faith, just as a friend? Not because you *liked* her?"

Willie shook his head as though he couldn't believe just how stupid I was.

"Josh, you don't just share your faith with girls you want to go out with." Willie couldn't hide his grin, even though he was a bit impatient with me. "I brought Mary to the Youth Group because she is a great girl, a good friend—one who has never really had a chance. She never attended church. Never got to spend time with those of us from the church. How else was she going to hear?"

"I just thought—" I interrupted. "Well, everyone thought that you liked Mary—special like."

"I couldn't court a non-Christian girl, and you know it, Josh. You know that God wants me to be a missionary. How could I be a missionary if I went and got sweet on a girl and married her and she didn't even share my faith? Why—"

"I had thought of it," I admitted. "It didn't make much sense to me either."

We sat in silence for a few minutes and then I dared to say, "Well, she's a Christian now, so if you decide you do like her—no problem."

Willie stepped from the swing, making it stop with a jarring movement. His hand reached up to smooth back his hair. I recognized the movement as one of exasperation.

"Okay, okay," I said quickly before Willie had a chance to speak. "So she stays a friend."

I got off the swing too and started back to the house.

"I guess I'd better get back to the books," I said defensively. "Only two more exams left."

Willie grinned. "I know. You want to get a 99 again."

I blushed.

"Where's it taking you, Josh?" asked Willie.

"What?" I stopped and eyed Willie.

"I shouldn't have asked it like that," continued Willie. "I didn't mean it to sound that way. I was just wondering if you knew something that you were holding back. Thought maybe you were trying for admittance in some super college where you needed great marks or somethin'."

I shook my head. I hadn't even applied to any colleges.

"You still don't know?"

I shook my head again.

"I'll keep praying for you, Josh," Willie said, slapping my shoulder.

"Thanks." I headed back to my bedroom and the open textbook.

I envied Willie. He already knew exactly what God wanted for him. He had no problem figuring out what to do in order to prepare himself. He could just plunge right on, getting himself ready for the task.

When graduation finally did arrive, I felt all strange. On the one hand I was excited about having completed high school. There were some awfully nice and embarrassing things said about me at the ceremony, too. I noticed Aunt Lou straighten in her chair and slightly lift little Sarah Jane so that she wouldn't miss any of the compliments. I could see the grins on the faces of Grandpa and Uncle Charlie, too. Grandpa was fairly busting his buttons. So I felt a measure of honest pride myself.

On the other hand, I felt all empty inside. Here I was, finishing up my schooling without the faintest notion of what I was to do next with my life. As I already said, Willie was going off to train as a missionary; Camellia was going to New York; Janie and Charlotte were both setting out to be teachers; Avery was going to work with his pa; Polly was getting married—the list could go on and on. But Joshua Jones, head of the class, didn't have any idea of what he would do with all this education.

I still felt all mixed up when we got back to Aunt Lou's and she served punch and cake in my honor to a number of friends and our family. She bustled around, chatting about me as she served, and Grandpa boasted some and Uncle Charlie just sat in the corner, quietly rubbing his knotted hands together as he grinned my way now and then. I could see, even then, that Uncle Charlie's hands were giving him pain again, but he, as was his way, didn't make any mention of the fact.

Over and over the question of my plans came up. I brushed them aside with comments such as, I was still "sorting it through" or "looking at possibilities" or "waiting to make a decision." Grandpa and Aunt Lou strengthened my position—"Lots of time," they'd say, or, "Josh has too much at stake to decide hurriedly." It made it sound like I had all kinds of choices.

In our private conversations they had already informed me that I shouldn't rush into deciding, should take my time and consider carefully the field that I wanted to pursue or the job that I would consider of interest, as God directed me. I knew that they were all still praying. I knew that they were all behind me, but I was quite sure that none of them knew just how much the question of the future weighed on my mind.

"You can stay right here and find a job in town until you decide what God wants you to do," Aunt Lou assured me. "We won't need the bedroom for Sarah Jane for a long time yet."

And I guess that was what everyone expected me to do. I had already had offers to work in the hardware store and the print shop. I was deeply thankful for the opportunity of choice but neither job really appealed to me.

So this was *my* reception—*my* time of honor. People came and went, giving well-wishes and enjoying Aunt Lou's refreshments and the friendly conversation. There was talking and laughter and a great deal of commendation. I tried to be a part of it, but my eyes kept straying back to Uncle Charlie and his bent shoulders and gnarled hands.

Suddenly something became very clear to me. As soon as I could, I excused myself and went to my room. I began to pack my few belongings into my duffle bag. It was spring. Planting time. I could see by Uncle Charlie's hands that he was in no shape to hold the reins. Grandpa would never be able to do all the planting alone. They needed me at the farm. The sorting out of my future could wait for now. I inwardly thanked God for putting it off for a while. We could work it out later, the two of us; but for right now I had a job to do.

I hurried faster as I packed, the emptiness within me filling up with anticipation. I loved the farm. I'd plant this one crop before I moved on. There wasn't time now to get any other help for Grandpa, and he needed his crop. If I didn't help him, who would? Scripture did say, after all, that we are to honor our parents. Grandpa wasn't really my parent, but he was the only father I had ever known. I figured that was what God meant when He spoke the words.

I sure would miss Aunt Lou and Uncle Nat, and I would dearly miss little Sarah, but I'd be nearby and able to see them often. God could have asked me to go to some far-off college or to a job in some distant town. Then I wouldn't get to see them at all. This was better—much better, for now. The decision felt right to me; and I had the impression that God approved of it. I was glad that I would have this extra time with family.

It was quiet again when I came back out to the kitchen. Grandpa and Uncle Charlie were just getting ready to head for home. They looked a bit surprised to see me out of my Sunday suit and into my everyday clothes. They were even more surprised to see my duffle bag.

"Mind if I throw my things in the wagon?" I asked. "I'll ride Chester."

"Sure," said Grandpa agreeably. "You plannin' on doin' some of yer sortin' out at the farm, eh?"

"No sortin' to be done," I answered him evenly. "At least not for the time being. Right now we got a crop to plant, and I aim to help."

"But what about a job—the further education?" Grandpa puzzled.

"We'll handle all of that when the time comes," I answered confidently. And the funny thing was, I felt confident. Uncle Nat had continually been trying to tell me that God would lead me. He would show me what I needed to know in plenty of time to do it. For me, right now, it was to help Grandpa and Uncle Charlie. That was all that I needed to know.

There were expressions of surprise on the faces before me, but gradually, one by one, heads began to nod assent.

"We're going to miss you," Aunt Lou whispered as she moved close to me and let her hand linger on my arm.

"That's the joy of it," I said. "I'll be nearby. I'll need to come to town often. Got to check up on Sarah, you know." We all laughed a bit and the tension in the room relaxed.

Grandpa and Uncle Nat helped me to load my things in Grandpa's wagon. I left nothing behind; I wanted no excuses for turning back. I went in to where Sarah was sleeping and gave her a little pat as I whispered a goodbye. Then I hugged Aunt Lou and Uncle Nat and scooped up Pixie.

"You ride with Grandpa and Uncle Charlie," I told her, and handed her to Uncle Charlie.

"I'll be along shortly," I promised them. "I'm just going to drop around and thank Mr. Lewis and Mr. Trent for their job offers and tell them that I'm needed on the farm—for now."

I don't know if I imagined it or not, but Grandpa seemed to walk with a lighter step and Uncle Charlie with a bit more straightness to his back as the two of them went toward the wagon.

Chapter 6

Farming

Thoughts about my future sometimes tugged at me as I prepared the ground for seed and planted the crop that spring, but for the most part I enjoyed what I was doing.

I had never had much to do with the planting before. Grandpa and Uncle Charlie had been in charge of that and I had been the chore-boy, but now the roles were reversed. Grandpa and I worked the fields and Uncle Charlie, in his own slow way, did the chores—at least most of them. I still did the milking, because Uncle Charlie found the job too difficult with his crippled hands.

Uncle Charlie took care of the household duties, too. Cooking and cleaning didn't seem to bother him too much, but scrubbing the weekly laundry sure did. I sometimes winced as I watched him trying to wring out a garment. That night, to get Grandpa alone I asked him to come with me to the barn to check old Mac's hoof. "What seems to be the trouble?" Grandpa asked, bending over to lift Mac's right front foot.

"Oh, no trouble," I quickly assured him. "I was just wondering if it should be trimmed just a bit more."

Grandpa looked disgusted for a moment, but he quickly caught himself.

"Boy, you are taking your farmin' serious, aren't you?"

he commented. "Never seen anyone with so many questions."

It was true. I had been asking a lot of questions. There were so many things that I didn't know about farming and planting, and I had to learn somehow. Grandpa and Uncle Charlie seemed to be my only source of knowledge.

"That's not—not really what I wanted," I began. "I wanted to talk to you, and I didn't know how to do it without Uncle Charlie—"

"Anything you got to say to me you can say in front of Charlie," Grandpa said firmly; I could tell by the tone of his voice that he wanted that straight right to begin with.

"But it's *about* Uncle Charlie," I protested. "Doesn't seem right to talk about him right out."

"What about Charlie?" asked Grandpa cautiously. "Seems to me he does the best he can."

"That's it exactly," I quickly pointed out. "He tries so hard, but some things are so—so difficult for him."

"Like?" asked Grandpa.

"Like wringing out those clothes."

Grandpa thought on that. He too had seen Uncle Charlie struggling with the clothes.

"Don't know what can be done about it," he said slowly and moved away from old Mac, slapping him playfully on his full rump as he did so. "Neither you nor I can take time to do the laundry when we're planting," he went on.

"I know, but—" I crossed to a wooden bucket and upended it to make myself a stool. "I've been thinking, and it seems that it might be the right time to get us some more modern equipment."

"Modern equipment?" Grandpa had always scorned anything that was too mechanized.

"One of those new machines for washing clothes," I hurried on. "They have a wringer thing that you just put the clothes through and turn the handle and they squeeze all of the water out from the cloth."

Grandpa knew all about washing machines. They had

been around for a number of years. He had just felt that they were unnecessary—up 'til now.

I waited. I had more sense than to press the issue. Grandpa stood there chewing on a straw and thinking.

"Lou has one," I finally mentioned.

"Lou needs one," said Grandpa. "She's got all those white shirts and fancy dresses and dozens of diapers."

"Lou had a machine long before she had diapers to wash."

"It work good?" Grandpa surprised me by asking.

"Real good," I answered. "I've used it myself. You just stand there—or even sit, and work the handle back and forth, and the agitator does the washin' of the clothes. Then when you've washed them long enough, you put them through the wringer and rinse them in the rinse tubs, wring them out again and you're done."

Grandpa took the straw from his mouth and teased one of the barn cats with it. It batted and swatted, enjoying the fun but never able to hit that straw. Grandpa always moved it just a bit too soon.

"I'll think about it, Boy," said Grandpa. "Might bear some looking into."

That was as close to consent as I expected Grandpa to come to right off.

There were other changes I felt needed to be made on the farm, but I reminded myself that it would be smarter to take them one at a time. For now the most important one seemed to be to get Uncle Charlie some help with that washing.

We headed back to the house then, both of us studying the evening sky to see if we could read what kind of a day we would have on the morrow.

"How's that east field coming?" Grandpa asked.

"Should finish tomorrow," I answered, "if the weather holds."

"Looks good," said Grandpa, his eyes back to the sky. "We're getting the sowin' done in time. Should have a fair crop."

When we reached the house Uncle Charlie was still puttering with the supper dishes.

"How's Mac?" he asked.

"Nothin' wrong with Mac," Grandpa answered easily. "Josh here did ask if his hoof needed a bit more trimmin'. But it was really just a ruse."

When Uncle Charlie looked up, I avoided his eyes and washed my hands so that I could wipe the dishes.

"He was really worried about other things," went on Grandpa. "Hates to see you wringing out those clothes on washday. Thinks you need one of those fancy machines."

I cringed. The way Grandpa was putting it, it sounded like I was making Uncle Charlie out to be some kind of sissy. I hadn't meant it that way at all, and if Uncle Charlie took it that way, he'd buck the whole idea.

"I've thought about that myself," said Uncle Charlie slowly. "Watched Lou use hers. Seems like a sensible gadget."

Grandpa just nodded like he wasn't surprised at all.

"Josh says that it is," he informed Uncle Charlie. "Guess we should look into gettin' one. We got the money for it?"

Now Grandpa had never concerned himself much with the day-to-day expenses of the farm and house. That was Uncle Charlie's job. You couldn't really say that he kept the books. There were no books involved, but Uncle Charlie always knew to the penny just where the financial matters of the household stood.

"Guess we've got the money if we decide we want one," he answered honestly. "Happen to have a bit extra right now. We had talked about adding some new hogs to the pen—"

"That can wait," said Grandpa.

"Suppose we'd have enough to do both," went on Uncle Charlie, "but hate to get too low just in case somethin' should happen to this year's crop. We get hail or anythin', and it might make it tight."

Uncle Charlie went on washing dishes and I began to dry them and place them back in the cupboard.

"We don't want to be short," Grandpa said emphatically. "No sense doin' that. We can wait on those new hogs."

In all my years of living at the farm I had never heard Grandpa and Uncle Charlie discussing finances as openly as they were now.

"We've got what we laid aside for Josh," went on Uncle Charlie. "Now that he's not heading right off to college—"

But Grandpa interrupted him. "He still might go this fall, and we sure don't want to be short of funds. We'll just leave that right where it is for now."

"We've got our savings—"

"We're not touching a penny of that," Grandpa said adamantly. "We worked hard to earn it and we sure aren't gonna go spend it."

Uncle Charlie nodded in agreement. It was the first I had heard of savings, or of the money for my further schooling.

"How much does one of those there machines cost?" asked Grandpa.

"Dunno," said Uncle Charlie. "I'll check next time I'm in town."

They seemed to have forgotten all about me. I dried the dishes and rattled them a bit as I put them back on the shelf. That didn't seem to work so I cleared my throat. They still ignored me.

"If you find out that it's what you want, just go ahead and order one," Grandpa was telling Uncle Charlie. Uncle Charlie nodded.

"How long do you think it'll take to come?" Grandpa pulled back a kitchen chair and sat down, removing his work boots and pushing his feet into his slippers.

"Dunno," said Uncle Charlie again.

I cleared my throat again. I had been there when Uncle Nat had ordered the machine for Aunt Lou. I knew what he had paid and how long it had taken to come, too. But I wasn't being asked and I hated just to butt in.

"Throat botherin' you, Boy?" asked Grandpa.

I shook my head, feeling a bit annoyed and embarrassed.

Uncle Charlie turned to me then.

"Do you recollect what Nat paid for Lou's machine and how he went about choosin' it an' all?" he asked me.

By the time I finished telling what I knew, Grandpa and Uncle Charlie had picked the make they wanted and decided that Uncle Charlie would head for town come morning and order himself a washing machine. I felt good about it as I headed up to bed. I had initiated one small change for improvement on the farm.

Chapter 7

More Decisions

I was so busy that spring and summer I scarcely even got to town. If it hadn't been for Sundays, little Sarah Jane would have grown up without me even seeing her. As it was, she seemed bigger and stronger and a little more attentive each time I saw her.

She soon learned to smile when she was talked to and to coo soft little bubbly noises. Soon she was content to lie there and talk. Her dark hair got lost somewhere, and when her new hair thickened and lengthened, it was a soft golden brown. Her eyes changed, too; they weren't as dark now and were showing definite blue.

As Sarah was growing physically, Mary was developing spiritually. Willie still picked her up for church, but now he was bringing her ma along, too. Mary was really excited about that, and Mrs. Turley seemed to enjoy the church services.

Willie was all excited about leaving in the fall for school. He kept getting letters telling him about the courses and what he was to bring, and every time he got one he'd rush right over and show it to me. He'd usually bring it out to the field where I was planting or cultivating or cutting hay.

We kept talking about fishing but we never did get around to going. There was just so much to do that we never had time. When I finished one job I was already behind in taking on the next one. I hadn't realized that farming kept a man so busy.

Grandpa said I should slow down a bit, but I kept seeing things that needed to be done. I hadn't been around long before I realized that some areas had been rather neglected in the last few years. I guess the farm had become too big a job for Grandpa and Uncle Charlie. I could remember a time when neither of them would have let such things go unattended.

Aunt Lou and Uncle Nat were pretty busy with church affairs and didn't get out to the farm too often. One Friday night they joined us for supper, and Aunt Lou did the cooking. Boy, was it good, too. Uncle Charlie did his best, but his meals were mostly boiled potatoes and meat.

"How's the work coming, Josh?" Uncle Nat asked after I had finished off a second piece of lemon pie.

"Good," I said, feeling kind of grown up and important. "We're haying now."

"How's it look?" Uncle Nat had been in a farming community long enough to know how important a good hay crop was.

I sobered a bit then. "Not as good as I had hoped," I said honestly. "Don't really understand. We got lots of rain, but it still looks a bit skimpy."

Grandpa entered the conversation then. "Soil's getting a bit tired," he offered. "It's been planted for a lot of years now. That hay field has been givin' us a crop for nigh unto forty years, I guess. Deserves to be tired."

"Could you use some help tomorrow?" Uncle Nat asked. "I could spare the day."

"Sure," I grinned at him. "I sure could use someone on the stack."

"I'll be here," he promised.

"I'll send the lunch," promised Aunt Lou. "I'll need to get rid of the rest of this chicken somehow."

I looked forward to the next day as I climbed the stairs to my room that night. It would be good to have Uncle Nat's help. But more than that, it would be good to have his company.

The day was a hot one; both Nat and I sweated in the midmorning sun.

When it was time to take a break for lunch, we decided to slip into the shade of the trees on the creekbank to have our meal. We gave the horses a drink from the stream, then tied and fed them and lowered ourselves to the cool grass in the shade of a large poplar.

After Uncle Nat asked the blessing on the leftover chicken and Aunt Lou's other good things, we chatted small talk for several minutes. At length Uncle Nat looked directly at me and asked candidly, "How's it going, Josh? You liking being a summer farmer?"

"Sure," I answered. "Like it fine."

"Are you any nearer an answer?"

I hesitated. "You mean, about what I should do?"

Uncle Nat nodded and I shook my head.

"Still bother you?"

"I guess it does," I answered honestly. "If I let myself think on it, it does."

"You planning to go to school somewhere this fall?"

"That's the problem," I said quickly. "I'd thought that I'd just come on out and help Grandpa get the crop in and then I'd stay long enough to help with the hay. But as soon as haying's over it'll be time to cut the green feed, and then harvest—and on and on it goes. There doesn't seem to be a good time to leave."

Uncle Nat nodded.

"Another thing," I said confidentially. "Things need a lot of fixing up around here. I hadn't realized it before, but I guess farming is getting too hard for Grandpa and Uncle Charlie." I hoped with all of my heart that Uncle Nat would understand my meaning and not think I was being critical of the two men. After all, I was still smart enough to know that they knew far more about farming than I did.

"I'd noticed," said Uncle Nat simply.

I took heart at that and dared to go on. "This hay crop,

for example. I think Grandpa is right; the land is tired. But it's gotta do us for years and years yet. There isn't any more land than what we've already got, Nat. We've gotta make this do for all the years God gives us. What do we do about it? Do we just wear it out?"

It was a hard question, one I had been thinking on a good deal lately.

"There are ways to give it a boost," said Uncle Nat, reaching for another sandwich.

I perked up immediately.

"Like what?"

"Well, not being a farmer I don't know much about it," Uncle Nat went on, "but I know someone who does."

"Who?"

"There's a fella by the name of Randall Thomas who lives about seven miles the other side of town," went on Uncle Nat. "I was called out there to see his dying mother. She wanted to talk to a preacher. Don't know why. She had things to teach *me*. A real saint if ever I met one."

I wasn't too interested in the saintly woman who probably had gone Home to glory by now. I wanted to hear about the farmer.

"Well, this farmer has been busy studying all about the soil and how to —what did he call it?—'rotate' crops to benefit it. Real interesting to talk to."

I was all ears. So there *was* a smarter way to farm the land!

"You think he'd talk to me?" I asked, very aware of the fact that I was still only a boy in some folks' thinking.

"I'm sure he would. Said if there was ever anything that he could do for me in return for calling on his mother, just to let him know."

I took a deep breath.

"So when do you want to see him?" asked Uncle Nat.

"Well, I don't know. Hafta get the hay off, and then the green feed—"

"And then the harvest," put in Uncle Nat.

"But I would like to talk to him," I continued. "I'd like to get the crops planted right next spring an'—"

Uncle Nat was looking at me.

"So you plan to farm again next year?"

I shrugged. "I guess so. I mean, I still don't know what else I'm supposed to do, and Grandpa still needs me an' . . ." It tapered off. There was silence for a few minutes and then I found my voice again.

"Do you think I'm wrong? Do you think that I should be tryin' harder to find out what God wants me to do with my life? It's not that I don't want to know, or don't want to obey Him."

"Are you happy here?" Uncle Nat asked me again.

"Yeah, I guess I am."

"You don't feel uneasy or guilty or anything?"

"No." I could answer that honestly. I was still puzzled, still questioning but I didn't feel guilty.

"Then, Josh, I would take that as God's endorsement on what you are doing," said Uncle Nat. "For now, I think you can just go ahead and keep right on farming. If God wants to change your direction, then He'll show you. I'm confident of that."

It sure was good to hear Uncle Nat put it like that.

We tucked away the empty lunch bucket and moved to the creek for a drink of cold water.

"And, Josh," said Uncle Nat just as we turned to go for the horses, "while you are here, you be the best farmer that you can be, you hear? Find out all you can about the soil, about livestock, about production. Keep your fences mended and your buildings in good repair. Make your machines give you as many years of service as they can. Learn to be the best farmer that you can be, because, Josh, in farming, in preaching, in any area of life, God doesn't take pleasure in second-rate work."

I nodded solemnly. I wasn't sure how much time God would give me to shape up Grandpa's tired farm before He moved me on to something else, but I knew one thing. I would give it my full time and attention until I got His next signal.

Chapter 8

Sunday

Willie came over to say goodbye before boarding the train that would take him away from our small community to the far-off town where he would continue his education. He was so excited that he fairly babbled, and for a moment I envied him and his calling. I would sure miss him, I knew that. It wouldn't be quite the same without Willie.

"You'll write?" Willie asked.

" 'Course I will."

"I'll send you my address just as soon as I'm settled," he promised.

"Let me know all about your school."

"I will. Everything," said Willie.

"What happens now—with Mary?" I asked suddenly, feeling concern for Mary and her mother.

"What happens? What do you mean?"

"For church? How will they get to church?"

"Mary is going to drive. I suggested that you might not mind picking them up, but Mary insisted that she'd drive them."

"Good," I said, and then hastily added, "but I sure wouldn't have minded taking them."

"I was sure you wouldn't, but Mary is quite independent."

We were quiet for a few moments; then Willie broke the

silence. "Take care of her, Josh. She's a pretty special person."

I looked at Willie, my eyes saying, "I told you so," but Willie didn't seem to catch the look.

"She's my first convert, you know," he went on, and then added quietly, "She often surprises me. She knows some things about being a Christian that I still haven't learned in all my years of trying to live my faith."

I nodded. Mary certainly was putting many of us to shame.

"I saw Camellia off yesterday," Willie said, and my head jerked up. I had hoped to learn of Camellia's parting date so that I could see her off myself, but I had been so busy with the farm. A funny little stab of sadness pricked at me somewhere deep inside. I couldn't even answer Willie.

"She sure was excited," Willie went on.

Yes, Camellia would be excited.

"Her pa seemed excited too, or proud or something, but her ma didn't seem to be too sure that they were doing the right thing."

I wanted to ask Willie how Camellia looked, how she was wearing her hair, what her traveling dress was like, all sorts of things so that I could sort of picture Camellia in my mind, but I didn't.

"She had more trunks and baggage than would be necessary for ten people," Willie was laughing. "I think her ma even packed her a lunch."

I still said nothing, and Willie thought that I'd missed his point. "They feed you on the train, you know."

I hadn't known. I had never traveled by train in my life, but I didn't admit my ignorance to Willie.

"She hasn't decided if she will get home for Christmas," Willie went on, answering the question that was burning in my mind.

"Will you?" I asked, making it sound like that was the most important thing in the world to me at the moment.

Willie shook his head slowly. There was concern in his

eyes. "I wish I could, but it's far too expensive to travel that distance. I'm sure I will be ready for some familiar faces by then. Four months away is about long enough for the first time from home, don't you think?"

I nodded.

"Well, I'd best get going." Willie reached to shake my hand. I extended mine, and then we both forgot that we were grown men saying goodbye to each other. We remembered instead that we were lifetime buddies, and the months ahead would be very long. Before I knew it we were soon giving each other an affectionate goodbye hug.

After Willie left I tried to get back to work in the field, but it was hard. Seeing my best friend riding off down the road, knowing that he would soon be on his way to Bible school, gave me an empty feeling in the pit of my stomach. Besides, Willie's news that Camellia had already left on the train for New York without my having the chance to tell her goodbye didn't do much to cheer me up. I had never felt so lonesome in all my life.

It wasn't long until Willie's first letter arrived. He was so full of excitement that he wrote pages and pages. I read it over and over, trying to get the feel of how it would be to be away from home.

I wasn't expecting any letter from Camellia, though I would have welcomed one. I did take a bit of a walk one Sunday while the rest of the family lingered over another cup of coffee after Aunt Lou's dinner. I went by the Foggelsons', hoping that I might accidentally meet Camellia's mother. It took quite a while and quite a few trips past their place, but eventually I did see her. She was watering her marigolds and I tipped my hat and greeted her like a mannerly boy was supposed to do. Then I casually asked her about Camellia.

Tears came to her eyes and she fought to control them. It frightened me. For a moment I was afraid that something dreadful had happened to Camellia, but when she spoke I realized that it was just the loneliness of a mother for her child.

She tried to smile.

"She is very excited about—about being on her own and the city and her classes and new friends." Then she added thoughtfully, "She—she hasn't said so, but even though she sounds cheerful, I think she has been just a bit lonesome."

The tears came again and Mrs. Foggelson attempted to smile in spite of them.

"I hope she is," she said wistfully, as though to herself. "I am."

I waited for a minute and then asked the question that I had really come to ask.

"Will she be home for Christmas?"

"No. Her father decided that she needs to make the adjustment to being on her own, away from family. It's much too far to travel, he says. I suppose he is right, but— Oh, my! How I dread the thought of Christmas without her!"

I was surprised somewhat that Mr. Foggelson, who doted on his only daughter, could consider Christmas without Camellia.

Mrs. Foggelson continued. "Mr. Foggelson needs to make a business trip east the last week of November. He will travel on to New York and take Camellia's gifts, and check to see how she is doing. He says that's quite enough."

My feelings for Mr. Foggelson hit an all time low. He had always felt that Camellia was his individual possession, but how could he do this to the girl's mother? And her friends? And how could he do it to Camellia? If she was really homesick, did he think that the sight of "dear old dad" was all she needed?

I couldn't even speak for a few moments. The angry thoughts were churning around inside of me. I looked away from the tears in Mrs. Foggelson's eyes and studied the distant maple tree, its bare arms empty as they reached upward against the gray autumn sky.

At last I found my voice. I even managed a smile. I guess

I felt more compassion for Mrs. Foggelson at that moment than I had ever felt before. This man, her husband, had robbed her of so much—her faith, her self-esteem, and now her only child. I wondered just what kind of account he would give before God on the Judgment Day.

I smiled and touched my hat again. "I'll keep in touch," I promised, and then stammered, "If that's all right."

"I'd love to see you, Josh. I need someone to talk to, and one of Camellia's friends would—"

She didn't finish, but I thought I understood. And her words, "one of Camellia's friends," echoed in my mind as I tipped my hat again and started back down the sidewalk toward home.

"Josh," Mrs. Foggelson's soft voice called after me.

I turned to look back at her.

"Keep praying—please," she almost pleaded.

I nodded solemnly and swallowed hard. I wasn't sure if she meant to pray for Camellia, or for herself, or that she would soon see Camellia again—or all three, but I'd pray. I'd pray lots and often. Living with a man like Mr. Foggelson, I felt that she really needed prayer.

I still hadn't controlled my anger toward Mr. Foggelson by the time I reached Aunt Lou's. I thought of walking right on by and spending some more time alone with my thoughts, but the realization that I didn't have too long until I'd need to go home for choring prompted me to turn into the yard.

Baby Sarah had just been fed when I reentered the house. She was in a happy mood, and Aunt Lou passed her to me, knowing that I would soon be asking for her if she didn't. She gurgled and cooed and even tried to giggle. Then she did the unforgivable. She spit up all over my Sunday shirt.

Aunt Lou jumped to run for a wet cloth, and Uncle Nat reached out to quickly rescue Sarah. I loved Sarah, but I sure did hate the feel and the smell of being spit up on. I guess I made some faces to show my disgust, and they laughed at me and ribbed me a lot.

Aunt Lou cleaned me up the best that she could, apologizing for the mess. She offered to wash my shirt, but I didn't have anything else along to wear and I figured I ought to be man enough to put up with a little bit of baby spit-up.

The need for laundering brought our thoughts back to Uncle Charlie and his washing machine.

Uncle Nat agreed to order the machine, and Grandpa and I both felt good about that. Now laundry wouldn't be quite so hard for Uncle Charlie—especially after my Sundays with little Sarah!

After a while I unobtrusively left the dining room and wandered down to the room that had been mine for so many years. The door was open, and it sure looked different. Aunt Lou had everything so neat and tidy, with new curtains on the window—white and frilly, not the kind of curtains a boy would have enjoyed. I had preferred my old tan ones, but these did look real nice. Little throw cushions were propped up against the pillows, too. I would have found them to be a nuisance.

I stood there for a few minutes looking around me and thinking back over the years; then I reached out with a toe and pushed the door shut. I knelt by the bed. "Father," I began, "you know how I feel about Camellia, and how sorry I am for Mrs. Foggelson. Well, I'm too angry right now to pray for Mr. Foggelson, but I do want to ask you to take care of Camellia and bring her into a relationship with Jesus . . ."

As I prayed for Camellia and her mother, my anger began to subside, and I began to realize how wrong my own attitude had been.

"Lord, Mr. Foggelson is a possessive and selfish man, and he's done some terrible things to his family. But I guess he needs you about as much as anyone I know. Help him find you too, Lord—and help me forgive him."

By the time I finished praying, I could think of the Foggelsons without feeling that turmoil of anger inside.

I rose and left the room, peeking into Aunt Lou and Uncle Nat's bedroom, where little Sarah now slept peacefully in her crib. She looked sweet, one little hand clutching the edge of her blanket and the other curled up into a tiny fist by her cheek. Her soft lashes against the pinkness of her skin looked so long and thick. Her hair, a little damp, curled closely to her tiny round head. It was getting lighter in color all the time; eventually it might be the same color as Aunt Lou's.

I reached down and smoothed out her blankets, then stroked the top of her head. She didn't even move. When Sarah slept, she really slept. Aunt Lou was thankful for that. There were many interruptions in the parsonage, and if the child had been a light sleeper, she might have never gotten a decent rest.

I heard stirring in the kitchen then and I knew that Grandpa and Uncle Charlie were preparing to leave for home. I whispered a few words to the sleeping baby and went out to get the team while they said their goodbyes.

Chapter 9

Winter

I was kept so busy that fall that I scarcely had time to miss Willie and Camellia. It seemed that I should have been in about three places at one time. There was so much to do, and only Grandpa and I to do the farming.

Grandpa had slowed down a lot, too. I hadn't realized until I was working with him just how difficult it was for him to put in a full day's work at the farm. I should have never left them alone while I went to school in town; I should have been there sharing in the responsibility. Maybe then things wouldn't have gotten so far behind.

But inwardly I knew that they never would have agreed to my staying at home. Even now, comments were made about my "calling" and I was reminded that I was not to hesitate when I felt God was prodding me on to what I "really should be doing" with my life.

I asked myself fairly frequently if I felt Him prodding, but I also found myself bargaining with Him.

"Can I wait, Lord, until I get the pasture fence mended?" I'd pray. "God, would you give me enough time to get in the crop?" And each time I asked His permission, I felt like I got His nod of approval.

Uncle Charlie's washing machine arrived in mid-October. I hadn't realized how much it meant to him until I watched him grinning as he uncrated it. He stroked the wringer lovingly, then gave it a few cranks and grinned some more. It was going to be a good investment.

The weather didn't cooperate that fall. The fields would dry just enough for us to get back at the harvest; we'd work a few hours, and then another storm would pass through, delaying us again. In my frustration I would go to fence-mending or repairing the barn or cutting wood for our winter supply.

I went to bed worn out every night and slept soundly until morning. Then I got up, checking the sky for the day's weather before I even had my clothes on, and started in on another full day.

It was late November before the district threshing crew moved in for the last time and we got the final crop off. Because of the rain, it wasn't as good a quality as we had hoped it would be, but at least it was in. Our hay crop of the year had been scant and poor, also.

Grandpa relaxed a bit then. The lines seemed to soften on his brow. Grandpa had too much faith for worry, but he was a little less concerned than he had been with the crop still in the field.

Uncle Charlie seemed to feel the lessening of tension too. For one thing, I knew that he was relieved to have his kitchen back to himself. We'd had a neighbor woman and her daughter in helping to cook for the threshing crew. Uncle Charlie needed the help, we all knew that, but he sure was glad when the last dish was washed and put away and the women went home.

I turned my attention to other things—cutting wood, fixing door hinges and banking the root cellar. And I talked to God some more.

I had thought I might be ready for His call at the first of the year, but now I realized that I would never be caught up enough to turn the farm back over to Grandpa and Uncle Charlie that soon. I needed more time to get things back into shape. God seemed to agree. I did not feel Him nudging me to hurry on other His plans. Instead, He seemed to give me assurance that my job on the farm wasn't finished yet.

And so I worked feverishly, trying to get as much as I could done before the snow came. When it did come, it came with fury. The thermometer dropped thirty degrees overnight, and the wind blew from the north with such intensity that it blew down several trees. The snow swirled in blinding eddies. I was thankful that I had repaired the chicken coop and lined the floor with fresh warm straw. I was glad, too, that the barn was ready for winter. But I still hadn't gotten the pigpens ready. I worried about the pigs, especially the sow that had just given birth to eight little piglets. I struggled against the wind with a load of straw for bedding.

It was useless even to try. The wind whipped the straw from my pitchfork as soon as I stepped from the barn. After trying several times, I tossed my fork aside and gathered the straw in my arms. Even that didn't work well. As I fought my way toward the pigpen the wind pushed and pulled, pulling the straw from me. By the time I had reached the pigpen I had very little left.

I tried again, over and over, and each time I arrived at the shed with only a scant armful of straw.

At last I gave up. I was winded and freezing as I bucked the strong gale. I hoped that the bit of straw I had managed to get to the pigs would help to protect them against the bitter storm.

I spent most of the day fighting against the wind, trying to ease the discomfort of the animals. Several times Grandpa and Uncle Charlie came out to assure me that I had done all I could, that the animals would make it through on their own. But I wasn't so sure, so I kept right on fighting.

When the day was over and I headed for the house with a full pail of milk, I was exhausted.

The kitchen had never looked or smelled more inviting. The warmth from the cookstove spilled out to greet me, making my face sting with the sudden heat after the cold. The odor of Uncle Charlie's hot stew and fresh biscuits reminded me of just how hungry I was.

Grandpa took the pail from me and went to strain the milk and run it through the separator. I didn't argue, even though it was normally my job.

Pixie pushed herself up against me as I fought with cold-numbed fingers to get off my heavy choring boots. She licked at my hands, at my face, anywhere that she could get a lick in. I guess it seemed to her that I had been gone for a very long time.

When I went to wash for supper, Uncle Charlie spoke softly from the stove where he dished up the food.

"Your face looks a bit chilled, Josh. Don't make the water too warm. You might have a bit of a frostbite there."

I felt my nose and my cheeks. They seemed awfully hard and cold. I heeded Uncle Charlie's advice and pressed a cloth soaked in cool water up against them. Even the cold made them burn.

Over the meal we discussed the storm and all I had done to try to prepare for it. I noticed that the woodbox was stacked high. Grandpa had been busy, too.

"Looks like it could be with us for a while," commented Grandpa. "Sky is awful heavy."

I didn't know much about reading storms, and I hoped that Grandpa was wrong. One day of this was enough.

We listened to the news on our sputtering radio while we warmed ourselves with coffee. The forecast wasn't good. According to the man with the crackling voice, the storm could get even worse during the night and wasn't expected to blow itself out for at least three days.

I could sense even before I awoke the next morning that the radio had been right. The storm was even worse than the day before.

When I went out to face the wind and the cold, the range cows were pushing tightly around the barn, bawling their protest against the storm. I knew that they needed shelter; I also knew that they could not all fit inside. The barn was

reserved for the milk cows and the horses. I felt sorry for
those poor animals. We really needed some kind of a shed to
protect them against such storms. *That's one thing I'll do
first thing next summer,* I vowed to myself.

The next day was a repeat of the two that went before it.
All day the wind howled. Then, near the end of the day the
wind abated and the snow slackened. The temperature
dipped another five degrees.

Even in the farmhouse we were hard put to keep warm.
Uncle Charlie lit a lamp and put it down in the cellar to keep
Aunt Lou's canned goods from freezing. We added blankets
to our beds and set an alarm so we could get up in the night
to check the fire.

The next morning arrived clear and deathly cold. The
water in the hand basin in the kitchen was skimmed with
ice. I lit the lantern and started for the barn, hating the
thought of going out to face the intense cold. My breath pre-
ceded me in frosty puffs of glistening white. Even the moon
that still hung in the west looked frozen into position.

Now that the wind had died down, I really had work to
do. The animals outside hadn't really eaten properly since
the storm had begun. It had been just too hard to fight the
wind. Now they stood, humped and bawling, hungry and
thirsty, and nearly frozen to death.

By the time the storm had passed and the temperature
was back to normal again, we had lost three of the piglets,
two of the older cows, and half a dozen chickens. Three cows
had lost the lower portions of their tails to frostbite, and our
winter supply of feed had already been seriously depleted. If
the winter continued this way, we would find it difficult to
continue feeding all of the stock. Even so, we fared much
better than some of our neighbors. The storm had killed a
number of the animals in some herds.

As Christmas approached, I was eager to spend time with
Aunt Lou and Uncle Nat. Little Sarah was sitting by herself
and even attempting to pull herself up. And the opening of

the Christmas gifts was, of course, even more fun with a baby in the house. We all had a gift for Sarah, and we took her on our laps and pretended that she was taking part in the opening of the present. We also pretended that she was excited about each new rattle or bib. She wasn't; in fact, she liked the rustle of the wrapping paper better than anything else.

I even brought Pixie with us. In the colder weather I usually left her at home when we went to town, but today I tucked her inside my heavy coat and she managed just fine. Sarah loved her, and I put Pixie through all of her tricks just to make Sarah squeal and giggle. She seemed to like it best when Pixie "spoke" for a little taste of turkey. Then Sarah would wave her chubby arms and squeal at the top of her voice. We all had a good laugh over it.

In the afternoon I slipped out and hurried over to the Foggelsons'. I wanted Mrs. Foggelson to know that I was thinking about her—still praying for her, too. Besides, I was a little anxious to hear any news about Camellia.

Before I went up their walk, I could see that there was no one home. The heavy curtains were pulled shut and no one had cleaned the snow from the walk for several days. The shovel was leaning up against the back porch, so before I headed home again I decided to clear the snow from the walk. I didn't know when the Foggelsons would be back again or if it would even be evident to them that someone had been there, but I did it anyway.

I wondered if there was some chance that Mr. Foggelson had changed his mind and they had gone together to see Camellia. I hoped so. It would be a lonely Christmas for both Mrs. Foggelson and Camellia if they were to spend it apart.

I thought of Willie, too. I had received a letter from him just a few days before Christmas. "I really miss the family and friends," he wrote. "As exciting as my studies are, I'm lonesome, even weary. But I've been invited home with one of the guys from the college who lives nearby." I was glad that Willie had somewhere to go.

When I was younger, I had always thought that as soon

as Christmas had come and gone, we should be working our way toward spring. I hoped that it would be true this year. I had loved winter as a boy, but then I hadn't had the responsibilities of seeing that everything and everybody made it through without mishap or suffering. Winter had simply been a time of sport—sleigh rides, tobogganing, ice skating, snowfalls and snowmen. I had loved it. Now winter was a time of struggle against the intense cold, the biting wind, the deep snow, the shortened days. The weather made it harder to chore, and the supply of winter feed and cut wood seemed to evaporate before my eyes.

Thinking of all this as I walked back to Aunt Lou's, I began to feel rather dejected. Then, it began to snow again—huge, soft, gently falling flakes. I looked up toward the sky to see the snow drift toward my face and marveled anew at the beauty of it. It might not be easy to live with winter, but it certainly was beautiful when I just took the time to look closely at it.

Chapter 10

Making It Through

I may have been ready for spring as soon as Christmas was over, but I guess no one thought to tell Mother Nature. She stormed and fretted and gave us a hard time all through the month of January. I looked forward to February—surely things would improve!

But they didn't. When we couldn't get to church a couple of Sundays, I missed the church service, the good dinner, and the brief visit with little Sarah.

And the bad weather didn't help Uncle Charlie improve, either. His arthritis seemed to twist his fingers off to the side more and more each day. I inwardly ached for him when I watched him trying to accomplish some simple task. But he was independent and needed to feel that he was carrying a full share of the workload.

About mid-February Grandpa came down with a bad cold. He struggled along trying to treat himself for several days but got no better.

"Grandpa!" I insisted. "You're just getting worse. I'm gonna fetch Doc to take a look at you."

"Bah!" he sputtered. "Doctors can't do nothin' I'm not already doing."

When it got worse and he had a hard time breathing, I

saddled Chester and headed for town—over Grandpa's pro-
tests.

"Sure enough," Doc murmured. "Pneumonia. You get
that girl of yours out here to take care of you 'til you get
back on your feet."

So Aunt Lou and Sarah moved out to the farm to nurse
Grandpa back to health. Doc had sent him to bed with orders
that he was to follow; Aunt Lou and I both knew he wouldn't
obey if she wasn't there to insist.

I was sorry that Grandpa was sick, but it sure was a treat
to have Aunt Lou and Sarah. Uncle Nat came out as often
as he could. He missed his "two girls," as he called them, but
he was awfully good about it.

It took Grandpa a couple of weeks before he was out of
bed, and even then he had to lie down often because he was
too weak to do much. In that time Sarah, crawling inces-
santly, had learned how to stand by herself. One morning I
came into the kitchen, and she deserted her toy to crawl to
me and pull herself up by my pantleg.

"Hey! You'll be running footraces soon!" She laughed,
bouncing up and down on pudgy baby-legs.

I was really sorry to see Aunt Lou and Sarah leave for
town again. The house would seem strange and empty with
them gone.

By March winter had still not given up, and we were short
of feed for the livestock. I worried about it each time that I
doled out the hay and oats.

Grandpa must have sensed it, mentally measuring the
feed each time I went out to chore. I didn't say anything to
him about it but one morning at breakfast he surprised me.

"About enough for two more weeks, eh, Josh?"

I nodded silently.

"Can you cut back any?"

"I think I've already cut back about as much as I dare."

"Any chance of buying some feed off a neighbor?" Uncle
Charlie asked.

"I've asked around some," I admitted. "Nobody seems to have any extra."

"We'll go out an' take inventory and see—" Grandpa started to say, but Uncle Charlie cut him short.

"You'll do nothin' of the sort!" he snorted. "Doc says yer to stay in out of the cold fer at least another two weeks."

"But Josh needs—" Grandpa began and Uncle Charlie waved his hand, sloshing coffee from his coffee cup.

"I'll help Josh," he said. "Nothin' in here that needs doin' today anyway."

Grandpa didn't argue any further, and after Uncle Charlie had washed up the dishes and I had dried them and set them back on the cupboard shelf, we bundled up and set off to take inventory.

It didn't take much figuring to know that we'd be short of feed. Uncle Charlie said what we were both thinking.

"If spring comes tomorrow it won't be in time."

By noon we had completed our calculations and headed back to the warmth of the kitchen. Grandpa had fried some eggs and sliced some bread. That, with cold slices of ham and hot tea, was our noon meal. I inwardly longed for Lou's full dinner meals again.

While we ate, Grandpa and Uncle Charlie juggled numbers and shuffled papers until I felt a bit sick inside. I wasn't sure where this all was leading us. I had never remembered a time when Grandpa and Uncle Charlie had had a tough time making it through the winter—but maybe it had happened and I just hadn't known.

In the end I was dispatched on Chester to take a survey among the neighborhood farmers. If there was any feed for sale, our dilemma would be solved.

But it wasn't that easy. Everywhere I stopped I found that the other farmers were in the same fix as we were. There just wasn't going to be enough feed to make it through this extra-hard winter.

With a sinking heart I headed for home. I decided to stop at the Turleys' on my way, more to see how Mary and her mother were doing than to check for feed. Mr. Turley fed several head of cattle and he didn't raise much more feed than we did.

When Mary opened the door, she looked genuinely glad to see me. I was even a bit glad to see her.

Mrs. Turley was busy darning some socks, and she sat there near the fire rocking back and forth as she mended. She seemed quite content and peaceful, even though she must have known that her husband, too, was facing a tough time.

"God will see us through, I feel confident about that," she assured me. "He always has—even when we didn't have enough sense to turn to Him—and I'm sure that He won't desert us now that we are His children."

My mouth must have gaped open at her words, for she looked at me and laughed softly.

"Don't look so surprised, young man. You young folks aren't the only ones who need converting, you know."

"Mother has become a believer, too," Mary whispered, a sense of awe filling her voice.

"Yes, praise God, thanks to the changes I saw in my Mary here, after she took up with your friend Willie—and his friend, Jesus."

"That's wonderful, Mrs. Turley," I stammered, still amazed at her words. "And you're right—we do need to trust Him."

Mary fixed some hot chocolate and cut some cake and we sat at the kitchen table and shared bits of news from the church and community. It seemed that she had chafed as much as I had over the snowed-in Sundays.

"Did you hear the Foggelsons are moving?" she surprised me by asking.

"They are? Where?"

"Mr. Foggelson has found a teaching position in a small college somewhere near New York. He went there to see about it in November and then he went back again over Christmas."

"Did Mrs. Foggelson go with him?" I cut in.

"No, he went alone."

"But she was gone—" I started to say, thinking back to the empty house and unshoveled walk.

"She went to her sister's. She didn't want to be alone."

"I don't blame her," I muttered, annoyed again with Mr. Foggelson.

"Camellia said her ma enjoyed her visit even if—" started Mary, but I cut in again.

"Do you hear from Camellia?"

"Oh, goodness no," she answered, shaking her head as though the thought were preposterous. "I hardly know her. I've just seen her on the street, and she would never have anything in common with the likes of me."

Then Mary blushed as though she were afraid that her words had somehow put Camellia down.

"I mean, well—we are—she's educated and all, and I—"

I rescued Mary from her embarrassment.

"Where did you hear about her?"

"From Willie. He wrote all about it. He keeps in touch with Camellia."

"Oh-h," I said. But it was rather an empty sound. I heard from Willie—often—but he had never informed me of all of Camellia's plans.

"Does Camellia like school?" I asked, because I was sure that Mary was expecting me to say something.

"Hadn't you heard?" asked Mary, taken aback. "She quit."

"Quit?" Now I was really surprised.

"She was only there for a couple of months when she quit."

"Then what is she doing? Why didn't she come home?"

"At first she was afraid to tell her pa. And then she left New York and managed to get some kind of job. A telephone operator, I think, out East. So she stayed."

What a disappointment that must have been for Mr. Foggelson. And then I thought of Mrs. Foggelson. She would

have been disappointed too, but not that Camellia had
dropped out of Interior Design. Her disappointment would
have been that Camellia didn't come back home.

"Well, Willie says that she likes her job just fine."

"So she writes to Willie?" For some reason, the news was
both encouraging and threatening at the same time. I wished
with all of my heart that Camellia felt free to write to me,
but at the same time I was glad that Willie was keeping in
touch. He had led Mary to become a Christian. Now it seemed
he was working on Camellia. Inwardly I prayed for Willie's
success.

But Mary was speaking again, with a bit of a laugh. "Oh,
she doesn't need to write. Her job is right there in town."

"Right where in town?" I asked stupidly.

"Where Willie goes to college. She is right there, working
on the town switchboard. Willie found the job for her."

Well, that was news to me. *Why hadn't Willie mentioned
it to me in one of his letters?* And then I smiled to myself.
Willie knew that I was already praying for Camellia. But he
didn't want me to get my hopes up too soon. Her father had
influenced her so strongly that it might take many weeks,
even months, before she would see the light after so many
years of antagonism toward Christianity, and I wouldn't ask
any questions of Willie. He'd share with me when he felt that
the time was right.

I suddenly realized that I had been sitting at Mary's table
for longer than I had intended. It was already getting dark
and there were chores to do. Besides, Grandpa and Uncle
Charlie would be anxious for my report—even if I wasn't
returning with good news.

"I've gotta get," I said to Mary and rose from the chair,
reaching for my coat and cap all in one motion.

Then I thanked her for the refreshments, told her mother
goodbye, and was on my way.

Mary saw me to the door.

"I'm sorry, Josh," she said quietly.

"About what?" I asked, startled.

"About the winter being so hard and all," she went on. "It's been a tough year for your first year farmin'—it was such a long, hard fall, and then—and then this," she finished lamely.

I was relieved at her words. I had been afraid that she had been going to say something about the Foggelsons. I had counted the days until Camellia would be done with her schooling and come back to our little town, and now with her folks moving, it didn't look like there was much chance of that happening. But I was relieved that Mary couldn't read my mind.

"Like your ma says," I returned, trying to sound brave and full of faith, "it'll turn out all right. God won't forsake us."

Mary gave me a big smile. She really had a very pretty smile, with white, even teeth and a dimple in each cheek.

I found myself smiling back. Maybe it was just that Mary's smile was contagious, or maybe I hoped she'd smile again. But for whatever reason, I did feel better as I mounted Chester and headed through the chilling weather for home.

Chapter 11

A Visit

We had to sell several head of cattle and all but two good sows. It would be a long time until we would get the herd and the pigpens built back up again, and I wondered if Grandpa and Uncle Charlie's decision was the right one. What if spring was just around the corner, and the new grass would soon be available? Maybe we would have been able, with careful rationing, to make it through.

It turned out that they had done the right thing. Another and then another storm struck, making it difficult to feed the few head of stock that remained. Neighbors who were trying to ration feed and make it through without selling off livestock lost most of their herd, and they didn't have cash from a sale to help them in rebuilding.

Our own stock diminished, and we lost one of our best milk cows when she got weak after giving birth to a fine calf. Grandpa and I sat all night with her, trying to keep her warm and pouring warm mash down her throat, but we lost her. I was sure we would lose the beautiful little heifer too, but Grandpa told me to carry her up to the kitchen, and Uncle Charlie took over from there. I don't know how he did it, but he pulled that little calf through. We all knew that she would be important in building up the herd again.

It seemed that all our days and nights were taken up with

fighting to save what Grandpa and Uncle Charlie had worked so many years to build. It just didn't seem right.

As soon as the weather began to warm some and I had a bit more time, I went off to town to see Uncle Nat.

"You know that fella you told me about who changes his crops around and such?"

He nodded. "Crop rotation."

"Yeah, rotation. Well, I was wondering if I might go and see him," I went on. "I've been wondering how he made it through the winter."

"Haven't heard," said Uncle Nat. "They mostly shop in Gainerville. Don't come here too often."

"Could you tell me how to get to his farm?"

Uncle Nat gave me directions. They sounded simple enough, and I headed Chester out of town. The day was bright, and the warmth of the sun shone down on the snow-banks. Chester was tired of winter and being shut up; he wanted to run, but I held him in check. I didn't want him to get all lathered up and then catch pneumonia. We had enough problems without losing Chester.

I found the farm without any trouble, though it took longer to get there than I'd thought it would. No wonder the family shopped in Gainerville—they were quite a ways from our small town.

Mrs. Thomas welcomed me cordially enough and informed me that her husband was down at the barn, so I declined her invitation into the kitchen and told her that I'd just go on down there to see him.

The Thomases were a big family. I saw three girls of varying sizes through the open kitchen door, and when I got to the barn there were four boys working along with their pa.

Randall Thomas was a big man, about forty, with a firm handshake and a kind twinkle to his eyes.

"Pastor Crawford's nephew, you say? Well, right glad to know ya, son," he said. "Sure did appreciate the trip yer uncle made out here to see Ma."

We chatted for a few minutes, my eyes traveling over the

barn and feed shed all the time I was talking or listening. It didn't look to me like there had been a feed shortage at this farm.

At last we got around to talking about the winter that we hopefully had just passed through.

"Sure a tough one," the big man said. "Worst I remember seein'."

I agreed, though it was evident that I hadn't seen quite as many winters as Mr. Thomas had.

"Looks like your stock made it through just fine," I said, nodding my head toward a corral holding some healthy looking cattle.

"Sold some of 'em way last fall," he surprised me by saying.

"You did?"

"Didn't want to wait until they only made soup bones," he went on. "A farmer has to think long-range. You figure about the worst that a winter can do to you and then plan accordingly. I figured out the feed I'd need to git each critter through to the end of May. By then the new grass should be helpin' us out some, even in the worst of years."

"We didn't have near enough feed to take us that far," I commented. "We had to sell several head."

"Too bad," he said sympathetically, shaking his head at our misfortune. "Heard some folks lost a lot of stock before they could even sell 'em."

"Grandpa sold early, before things got too bad," I informed him.

"That was smart thinkin'," went on the man. "The way I see it, a few real good, healthy head of stock are better'n a whole herd of weak, half-starved ones."

I could see his point.

"A herd can get themselves into pretty bad shape if you don't keep upgradin' 'em," he went on. "Then they can't take much cold an' poor feed."

I looked at his sleek cattle. They didn't look like they had just been through a tough winter.

A bird overhead drew my attention to the sky. The sun had already moved far to the west, losing much of the warmth of the day. It was a long ride back home, and I knew I should soon be making it.

"I really came to see you about your crops," I told Mr. Thomas. "I've a feeling that we would have fared much better this winter if our land were producing like it should be. Seems to me the hay that we took off was only about half as high or heavy as it could have been."

His eyes glinted with interest as they met mine.

"You just startin' to farm?" he asked.

I nodded, then corrected myself. "Well, I was raised on that farm but until this year I've been doin' the chorin', not the farmin'. Grandpa and Uncle Charlie have been farmin' the land. They aren't able to do it all now so—"

He cut in. "So you are farmin', and you wanta start out right?"

I nodded again.

"Well, yer a smart boy." His hand fell to my shoulder and he gave it a squeeze.

"A man can farm his land right out iffen he plants the same crop year after year. Only stands to reason. Why, even way back in the time of the Israelites, God gave a command that the land was to get a rest ever' now an' then. Same thing now. The land needs to rest—to build up its reserves agin." And then he began an enthusiastic explanation of how that was to be done.

I listened attentively. But the sun was moving on, and there was so much to learn. I felt frustrated and tense, and I guess that the man sensed it.

He stopped and his eyes followed mine to the sky. "There's too much to learn in one afternoon," he told me. "You come on back—as often as you like—and we'll pick it up from here."

I was glad he understood my need to be on the road and for the invitation to come to see him again.

"Tell ya what," he continued as we walked toward Chester. "You draw up a plan of yer fields. Mark what's been growing in each for the last seven, eight years, and then come see me agin. We'll see what ya should be plantin' come spring."

I could only stammer my thanks. I hadn't expected that kind of help.

"It's important to get good seed, too," the man continued. "Some farmers try to skimp on the cost of seed. But that costs 'em more than it saves 'em. Just like it is with livestock. The Bible says, 'Ya reap what ya sow.' Now I know that wasn't talkin' 'bout the grain and the stock as much as it was what ya sow in life, but the same holds true."

I hadn't thought of it that way before, but it made sense. It was a totally different approach to farming than I had been used to, but I promised myself that I would learn all I could about it. I thanked the man for his kindness and mounted Chester.

"Now that," he said appreciatively, running a hand over Chester's thick neck, "is good breedin'. Where'd ya get a horse like this, son?"

I explained that Chester had been a gift and reached down to rub his neck myself.

"First-rate horse!" the man exclaimed, making me beam with his praise.

On the way home I let Chester do a bit of running, though pacing him so that he wouldn't get too heated. But, like the man had said, Chester's good breeding showed. He could run a lot without getting winded or sweated up.

I had so much to think about that my head was swimming. Good seed, good blood lines, crop rotation—those were things that spelled out productive farming. And if a man was going to farm—even if it was just until God called him into his real life's work—then he ought to try to do a good job of it. I determined that I would find out all I could about doing the job right. Maybe the next time we had a bad winter we wouldn't need to suffer such serious setbacks.

Chapter 12

Looking for Spring

As my interest in farming techniques increased, I found some farm magazines with articles about crop rotation and pored over them. I sent away to the Department of Agriculture for free information that was mentioned in one of the magazines. I also asked them for information about building up the herd with proper blood lines. Soon pamphlets and sheets of information were coming back through the mail. I hadn't realized that there was so much to farming—or that the government had information available to help farmers. There were even agricultural courses that a fella could take at home. I had always thought that a man became a farmer because he had been born and raised on the farm and his pa needed help.

"You been gettin' an awful pile of mail lately," Grandpa remarked, glancing at the three brown envelopes and a magazine on the kitchen table.

"There's a lot more to this farming than I ever knew from just growing up on one," I commented. "You and Uncle Charlie made it seem so easy—"

"Oh, we did the best we knew how, and it worked pretty good most of the time," Grandpa interrupted, "but it looks to me like yer findin' some real important things 'bout farmin' in those magazines and booklets of yers. Charlie an' I've been readin' some of them, too," he said to my questioning look. "We're real glad yer learnin' some new ways to do things." From the shine in his eyes, I knew he meant it.

All through the chill of spring I worked with the stock, trying to keep them comfortably warm so their energy could be reserved for putting fat on their bodies. I still couldn't feed them the way I would have liked, but I made a warm mash for them on the cooler days, and kept the animals in the barns all I could. It meant more barn cleaning, but if the stock benefited, then it would be worth it.

On the sunnier days I let them out to pasture. The snowdrifts were slowly melting down and the horses led the way for the cattle, pawing back the snow in order to get to the left-over grasses from last fall. They even began to discover some fresh new blades of grass and that increased their desire to forage. The cows followed along behind, eating from the open spots the horses had left.

Every day I watched the sky, the snow patches, the weather, mentally measuring the feed I had left with the number of animals.

At night I read the magazines and information booklets, and I began to see what Mr. Thomas had been trying to tell me—there was a *system* to good farming.

I drew out a map of the fields, and Grandpa and Uncle Charlie and I went over them one by one. It was hard to remember every field back for seven or eight years. Sometimes Grandpa and Uncle Charlie disagreed about the crop that had been planted in a particular field and then they would have to sort through their thinking, trying to figure out which one was right. I decided then and there that an accurate account of each field would be kept year by year, along with the yield and any other information I might come up with.

Daily I checked my feed rations; I was still anxious that we wouldn't make it to the end of May. Finally we held a consultation and decided to sell off two more young heifers.

They looked small-boned, and we wanted to build up our herd with larger animals.

Instead of going to see Mr. Thomas alone, I suggested to Grandpa and Uncle Charlie that they come with me. I wanted them to hear firsthand what the man had to say, and to catch some of the excitement that he generated.

Thus on a mild day that held a promise of spring, we hitched the team to the wagon. The road was rutted and messy with dirty puddles of half-melted snow. The ground had not yet yielded up its frost, but still it was hard pulling for the team, and we didn't travel very fast. I drove and Uncle Charlie and Grandpa just sat there and soaked in the warmth of the sun. It had been a long time since they had been able to feel the sunshine.

It was just as I had hoped that it would be. We were welcomed with a handshake that made my hand tingle. I thought of Uncle Charlie and his arthritis and almost said something, but Mr. Thomas must have noticed the crippled hands, for he took my uncle's hand very carefully and didn't squeeze at all.

This farmer's enthusiasm was contagious. He talked about the importance of good seed, of planting in weed-free fields, of rotating the crops so that the soil wouldn't become depleted, and of fertilizing properly each year.

With the livestock kept in so much of the winter, at least we wouldn't be short of fertilizer. But I winced as I thought of the unpleasant task of scattering it over the fields.

With the help of Mr. Thomas, we analyzed our field situation and determined what crops should be planted where and which field should go fallow. The next step was to find a source of good seed grain. We were in the favored position of being able to afford a bit of good seed. Before we left, Mr. Thomas promised to come out and take a look at our livestock. He would help us sort out the best that we had and then figure out how to start developing better stock.

My head was whirling by the time we put down our coffee cups and headed home. We had so much to think about and so much to get done—even before planting time.

All the way home I was planning the days ahead. Even if spring was slow in coming, I still didn't think we'd be ready for it. There was so much to do to prepare the ground for the coming crop year.

Because I knew I would be more than busy once we could drive the wagon out to the fields, I decided to call on Mrs. Foggelson before I got too rushed. I was sorry to hear she would be leaving us. I guess I was even a little sorry to hear that he would be going. I wished with all my heart that he could realize that there was a God—a God who was in charge of the universe. How could someone with such a brilliant mind be so wrong about something so important?

With the move, I wouldn't be seeing Camellia again. I had hoped the day would come when both she and her mother would become believers. Mr. Foggelson, I knew, would be hard to convince after so many years of resisting the truth.

When I got to the Foggelsons' the snowbanks had almost disappeared off their front lawn. Little shoots of spring plants pointed up through the final snow covering the flower beds. I knew that Mrs. Foggelson dearly loved her flowers, and I wondered who would be caring for them after she had moved away.

In answer to my knock, Mrs. Foggelson came hesitantly to the door. When she saw me, her face lighted up and she flung the door open with a welcoming smile.

"Josh! So good to see you," she said, sounding glad that I had come. I sat twisting my cap in my hands in her parlor while she rushed to the kitchen for tea. Once we were settled with our cups, Mrs. Foggelson chatted about spring, about her garden, about the hard winter, and finally about Camellia.

"Did you know that Camellia quit studying Interior Design?" she asked. I had to admit that I did.

"Did you know that she is working as a telephone operator?"

I nodded again.

"I am so glad," went on Mrs. Foggelson. "I was so worried about her in New York. She got in with the wrong choice of friends almost immediately, and I was so worried."

I hadn't known about that.

"Does she like her work?" I asked.

"Not really. But it is good clean work with good people. That's the most important thing. Camellia might be smart, and she might be independent, but she has had no experience dealing with people. Especially the kind of people who would lead her into—into wrong living."

I hardly knew what to say. I just nodded my head in understanding, trying to balance the light flakes of pastry that didn't want to stay on my fork.

"I'm glad she's no longer in New York." Mrs. Foggelson sighed with relief.

I nodded again, then ventured, "But you must be sorry that she won't be close by when you move."

Her eyes dropped and she was silent for a few minutes. When she looked up again, her voice was very soft and low.

"I won't be moving," she said.

"There's been a change of plans?" I asked hopefully.

She just shook her head.

"But—but I was told that Mr. Foggelson got a teaching position in a small college—somewhere near New York City."

She let her eyes look evenly into mine.

"Yes," she said, "he did."

Silence.

"Well," I prompted, "then he has changed his mind after all."

"Oh no. He'll be going as planned."

"But—" I felt that we were talking in riddles. I stopped and waited for her to enlighten me.

"Mr. Foggelson will be going as he has planned," she said carefully, "but I will remain here."

I must have looked as shocked as I felt. I lowered my fork, scattering the last of my flaky pastry onto the white damask cloth. My face flushed hot with embarrassment.

Mrs. Foggelson reached over to pour me some more tea. I didn't have a voice to refuse it, even though I didn't think that I could drink another drop.

"Did you notice that the early tulips are already showing some?" Mrs. Foggelson asked, as though flowers were all we had been discussing since I had come in.

I nodded and cleared my throat again.

"I do so hope that we have a nice spring," said Mrs. Foggelson. "We can't have an early one—it's already too late for that, but I do hope it's a nice one. I am so tired of the dreary winter."

My eyes drifted to a picture of Camellia on the corner table. Mrs. Foggelson had lots of pictures of Camellia. Or were they Mr. Foggelson's? I looked about the room, my mind busy with embarrassing thoughts. Who would get the pictures? Who would get the brocade sofa? Who the silver tea service or the china cups?

What did folks do when they separated company, anyway? How did they ever go about portioning out a house? A home? I knew absolutely nothing about such things. But surely some rough days lay ahead for the Foggelsons.

Then another thought quickly came to my mind. With Mrs. Foggelson staying, maybe— "Does Camellia plan to stay on in the little town where she is, or—or might she come back home again?"

For the first time I saw the tears threaten to form. Mrs. Foggelson shook her head slowly, and suddenly her lovely, gentle face looked old.

"I don't expect so," she said candidly. "Camellia does not approve of my staying here. She has always been her daddy's girl, you know. If she goes to anyone, it will be to him."

I pushed back my chair and got to my feet. I felt so sorry for Mrs. Foggelson, but there was really no way I had of telling her. What could a young fella like me know about the way she hurt? How could I understand her reason for doing what she was doing? And yet, from the expression in her eyes I knew that her decision to remain behind was not made lightly.

"I'd best be going," I said hoarsely. "I still have things to do before I head for home."

She nodded in understanding and smiled. "You drop in anytime you can, Joshua."

I worried about her as I left. The tulips were appearing. Mrs. Foggelson would do just fine tending her beloved spring flowers. But who would be responsible for the many other things that needed tending?

The school year was almost over, and Mr. Foggelson would undoubtedly leave as soon as he was finished with his teaching obligation. That would leave Mrs. Foggelson totally on her own. She hadn't made many friends in town, either. She would need someone.

I had been brought up to not take kindly to neighborhood gossip, but I knew I had to talk to Aunt Lou. I knew she was busy with all her housework, the church, and baby Sarah, but Mrs. Foggelson would need some lady to talk to, and I figured that Aunt Lou would be just the one. I would help Camellia's mother all I could. I wouldn't be able to do much, but I'd pray. And I'd get Aunt Lou.

Chapter 13

Building

Days passed into weeks, weeks to months, and months to years. During those two years I worked hard, occasionally wondering if God would suddenly make up His mind about what He wanted me to do and move me on before I had things under control at the farm. If I had thought it through at the time, I would have realized that our heavenly Father doesn't do things that way.

With the help of Mr. Thomas, we got the quality seed that we needed and began our crop rotation. But there were no miracles. The land did not turn more productive overnight. By the end of the second year of our new program, Grandpa and I both hoped we were seeing some improvement in the yield—but maybe it was just that we had a wonderful summer for growing.

The herd, too, was slow to increase. We were able to purchase a few good animals from Mr. Thomas, and with the best from our own herd, we began to build for the future. But there were no quick profits on our investment, and we had to watch the farm budget carefully so we wouldn't overextend ourselves. The calves of that spring were the first real return we saw on our experiment; even Uncle Charlie had to come out to the barnyard to have a look as each one arrived. One of the cows had twins—both little heifers that would one day greatly strengthen our herd.

Aunt Lou's family was increasing, too. Jonathan Joshua joined Sarah at the parsonage. Sarah, at two years, was so excited that she could hardly contain herself. She called him "my brudder," and squeezed him each time she came near him. She wanted to share everything with him, from her fuzzy teddy to her breakfast toast. Aunt Lou had to watch her closely.

Willie came home the first summer, excited about how God was helping him with his studies and also his finances. He was just bursting with it all. But he ended up getting a summer job at Gainerville, so I didn't get to see him nearly as much as I would have liked.

He did talk with me about Camellia, however. She was still angry about her ma staying on in town. Willie said that Camellia had, at one point, become quite open and willing to listen to him as he tried to explain his faith. Then when she got the word about her folks, she completely turned it all off again. Willie said he didn't dare raise the subject after that. Everytime he attempted to say anything about Christianity, Camellia would remind him that her ma had at one time professed faith, and look what she had done to her pa. It wasn't fair of Camellia, we both knew, but people can reason in strange ways sometimes. Willie urged me to keep on praying, and I promised I would.

Mrs. Foggelson didn't stay on at the big house after Mr. Foggelson left town. She moved the few things that she still called her own into a single room at the boardinghouse in town and started to take in sewing. There were no silver tea services, no sets of fine china, no flower beds of tulips and roses—nothing but a sewing machine and the bare necessities of life.

But Aunt Lou did befriend her, and she responded. She often walked over to the parsonage for a cup of tea. Aunt Lou was even able to get her to start reading her Bible again— but she still wouldn't agree to come to church.

Willie didn't even come home the next summer. He had a job there near the school. I missed him, but I was really too busy to think much about it.

The harvest weather was better and the crops were in on time. The next winter was milder, too, and our few animals fared much better.

When spring returned, we planted again—this time with some of our own seed. We had chosen the best, spending many of our winter evenings gathered around the kitchen table carefully sorting out seed for planting. For Uncle Charlie it was difficult; his twisted hands found it almost impossible to handle small things.

That third year on the farm, the crop that we planted gave us the best yield we had seen for some time. The hay did especially well, and the pruned-back fruit trees began to bear again like they hadn't in years. We'd have several pigs ready for fall market, and the cattle, though slow to make a comeback, showed good quality in the small herd we were developing.

We were even able to put out money for paint, and in between the haying and the harvesting I was able to paint the buildings, including the house. It sure did make the whole farm look better.

I even began to think about a tractor, though I didn't mention it to Grandpa and Uncle Charlie. I knew they would be likely to think I was moving a bit too fast.

The crop was all in, and I had just celebrated my twenty-first birthday when I got a letter from Willie. We hadn't been writing quite as often as we once had, and I was pretty excited when I saw his handwriting. Willie was now in his final year at the college and would soon be a mission candidate. I knew he was excited about finding which foreign field God had in mind for him. I would have been excited too, but the thought of Willie graduating was a reminder to me that I was already four years behind in my preparation time. It would take a good deal of extra hard work once God showed me what He wanted me to do with my life.

I just had to write, Willie said, *and share with you the most exciting news. Camellia has become a Christian. I won't tell you any more about it than that, as she wants to tell you all about it herself when we come home for Christmas. Yes, you read that right. She is going to come home to see her mother. She knows that they must get some things straightened out between them.*

I couldn't believe it! It was just too good to be true. And yet I didn't know why I found it so hard to believe. I had been praying daily for several years for that very thing to happen. The tears began to fill my eyes, and I brushed them away with the back of my hand.

Camellia was a Christian! Camellia would be coming home at Christmas! It all seemed like a miracle. Praise God! Bless Willie!

I read on, the pages blurred now from the tears in my eyes.

We'll be there on Monday's train, Willie went on. *It arrives at 11:35 a.m.—or is supposed to. Remember how we used to go down to the station to watch for the train—not to see the train as much as to watch the people? Remember how some of them would get so irate because the train was always so late? Well, if it's that late on Monday, the 21st of December, I might understand for the first time why they acted as they did.*

My eyes slid to the calendar. The twenty-first was twelve days away. How would I ever be able to stand the wait?

Then I let out a whoop and raced the stairs two at a time to tell Grandpa and Uncle Charlie the good news.

Chapter 14

Sharing the News

I daydreamed my way through the rest of the day and tossed my way through the night. After such a long time, I would see Willie and Camellia again! Camellia had become a Christian!

The next morning I saddled Chester and headed for town. I couldn't wait to tell the good news to Uncle Nat and Aunt Lou.

Sarah saw me coming and met me at the door. "Hi, Unca Dosh!" she shouted before I even had time to dismount. She was still having trouble with her *j*'s. And I was still waiting for the day when she could properly say uncle, though I must admit that I secretly thought "Unca" sounded pretty cute.

I picked her up and gave her a kiss on the cheek. "Hi, sweets."

"Have you been to da store?" she asked coyly.

"No, I came straight here to see you." I kissed her cheek again. Sarah knew that only shopping brought us to town midweek.

She squirmed to get down and I set her on her feet.

"Can I go wif you?" she asked, her big blue eyes pleading.

"I don't need to go to the store this time," I replied, feeling quite flattered that she wanted to be with me every moment that I was in town. "See?" I continued, pointing to Chester,

107

"I didn't even bring the wagon—just Chester."

Sarah's lower lip came out, and I thought for a moment that she would cry.

"I'm not going to the store," I repeated quickly, crouching down to her level.

The tears came to her eyes then, and she looked at me as she tried to blink them away. "Then how can you get candy?"

For a minute I didn't quite understand. Then it dawned on me. We came to visit *after* shopping, and we always had a small bag of treats for Sarah.

I couldn't help but laugh. The little beggar hadn't done a great deal for my ego, but at least she was honest and forthright.

"No candy this time," I said, tousling her curly hair. "Too many sweets aren't good for you. Where's your mamma?"

"She's wif brudder." The tears were already disappearing.

"Where?"

"In the kitchen."

"Is she feeding him?"

"No," said Sarah, shaking her head, "baffin' him." Then she suddenly seemed to remember that she was missing one of her favorite parts of the day. She turned from me and ran back through the porch into the kitchen, calling as she ran, "Mamma! Unca Dosh is here."

"Good," Aunt Lou answered, "Come right on in, Dosh." I could hear the chuckle in her voice.

I wasn't really uncle to Sarah and Jonathan, of course—I was cousin. But Aunt Lou was training the children to call me uncle since our relationship fit with that title better.

Sarah ran ahead of me and climbed up on a kitchen chair beside the table before I got there.

"See!" she pointed excitedly. "Brudder can sit now."

I couldn't believe how much he had grown just since the last time I'd seen him.

Aunt Lou smiled at me. "I'll be done here in a second; then I'll fix you some—whatever you want. Coffee, tea, milk, lemonade."

I nodded, reaching to chuck Jon under the chin. "How ya doin', big fella?" I asked him. He rewarded me with a grin.

"He's got a tooth already!"

"Two," corrected Sarah. "Mamma say two."

"Two is right," informed Aunt Lou. "Another one is just coming through."

Aunt Lou finished dressing Jon and handed him to me.

"Will he spit?" I would have taken him even if she had assured me that I was bound to get spit up on.

"He's good about that," she said instead. "Hardly ever spits up. And I haven't fed him yet, so you're safe."

Sarah and I played with the baby while Aunt Lou made hot chocolate and cut some slices of lemon loaf. "So, how is everyone?" she asked.

"Fine."

With her question and my reply, my good news again came foremost in my thinking.

"Uncle Nat here?" I asked. I had hoped to tell both of them together.

"No, he went out to the Lewises'. Mr. Lewis is the new Church Board Chairman and they have some things to discuss."

I was disappointed, and it showed.

"Did you need him?" asked Aunt Lou.

"Oh no. I—I just got some great news, and I wanted to tell both of you."

Aunt Lou's head came up from the stirring of the hot chocolate. Her eyes searched mine. "Well, you aren't going to make me wait just because Nat isn't here, are you?"

I grinned. "Naw," I said. "I wouldn't be able to stand it."

"Good!" she said emphatically and set the two cups of hot chocolate on the table. Then she reached for a glass partly filled with milk for Sarah.

"So?" she asked, passing me the lemon loaf.

"Just got a letter from Willie," I began.

"Did he get his assignment?"

"Nope. Even better than that."

"He's coming home?" said Aunt Lou, knowing I would be pretty excited about that.

"Yeah, for Christmas—but there's more."

I was really enjoying this little game. We had played it many times over the years, savouring some bit of exciting news and making it stretch out just as much as possible.

"And?" prompted Aunt Lou.

"Camellia is coming, too."

"Camellia?" Aunt Lou sounded almost as excited as I had been.

I nodded, my face flushed with the wonder of it all.

"Here?"

"Here! To see her ma."

Aunt Lou surprised me then. She started to cry. I think she started to pray too. She was talking softly to someone, and I knew it wasn't me.

I sat there hardly knowing how to respond; then I got up from my chair and gently laid Jonathan in the small bed that stood in the corner of the kitchen. I had the feeling that Aunt Lou might need me, but I still didn't know just what move I should make. Sarah brought me back to attention. She reached for Aunt Lou's hand, concern in her eyes.

"Mamma," she said. "Mamma, why you cry?"

Aunt Lou's face changed immediately and reached out to gather Sarah to her. She began to laugh softly. "It's all right, sweetheart," she assured Sarah. "Mamma is crying for joy. I'm fine. Really. It's all right."

Then Aunt Lou turned to me. "Mrs. Foggelson will be so happy. I told her I'd pray that Camellia would forgive her for what she had to do."

Had to do? The words echoed and reechoed in my mind. But I didn't ask questions—at least not then.

Then Aunt Lou put a hand on my arm and, looking at me with tears starting again, pleaded, "Oh, Josh! We've got to pray like we have never prayed before. We've got to pray that this time together might be a time when Camellia and Mrs.

Foggelson will realize how much they need God in their lives."

"Well," I began, then abandoned all caution and rushed on, "that's the rest of the good news. Camellia has already realized that."

Aunt Lou's eyes got big and she searched my face to see if I had really said what she understood me to say.

"You mean—?" she began. I nodded and then I gave a whoop and reached out for Aunt Lou and we laughed and cried and praised together.

"I've gotta go," I said to Aunt Lou finally. "I really didn't have time for a trip to town today, but I just couldn't wait to tell you."

"Oh, Josh," she said, "I'm so glad you came. That is the most exciting thing that has happened since—since Jonathan," she ended with emphasis, and turned to her little son.

Jonathan sucked his fist noisily, reminding his mother that he was still unfed. Aunt Lou kissed his forehead and murmured something to him.

I heard a deep sigh from the chair beside me and looked down into the forlorn face of little Sarah. She sighed again, gave her little shoulders a shrug and turned her small palms up.

"Nonny sweets," she said. "Nonny" was Sarah's own word. As far as we could figure out, she meant "not any" or "none" when she used it.

Both Aunt Lou and I laughed.

"Here," I said, fishing in my pocket. "Here's a penny for your piggy bank."

Her face immediately lit up and she took the penny from me, scooted down from her chair and called as she ran toward her room, "T'anks you, Unca Dosh."

We heard the penny clink as it joined the others in her bank. I grinned as I shook my head.

"That's an awful little beggar you're raising there, Lou," I said.

"Me?" responded Lou. "*Me? Seems to me her begging has something to do with three men in her life.*"

I shrugged my shoulders, turned my palms upward, "Nonny sweets." I grinned and left.

Chapter 15

Homecoming

I suffered terribly waiting for the twenty-first. I kept trying to imagine what it was going to be like to see Camellia again. I wondered what the *new* Camellia would be like. She was a believer now. She would undoubtedly have a new softness, a new understanding, a new gentleness to her.

On the other hand, I hoped she hadn't changed *too* much. I would have been terribly disappointed if she had put her beautiful coppery hair into some kind of a tight bun or something. And I couldn't imagine her in strict, plain dresses either. Somehow they just wouldn't suit Camellia.

And Willie—it seemed like such a long time since I had seen him. He was bound to have changed. I thought I had grown away from Willie; that after my first awful months of missing him so, I had finally learned how to get along without him. But now that he was due home, all the old memories of our friendship returned, and I missed him more than I ever had.

A glance in my mirror told me that I had changed over the years, too. I tried to think back to how I had looked at eighteen and I couldn't really remember. I knew I had filled out since then. The clothes I had worn as a teenager just hung in my closet, waiting for someone to sort through them and discard them. But somehow it felt comfortable to have them still hanging there day after day, month after month, even though I knew I would never be able to wear them again.

I looked at my muscular arms. Shoveling the grain on the wagon and shoveling the fertilizer off had made me quite well developed, not the skinny teen I had been.

I rubbed the outline of my jaw. At seventeen I had shaved a few times, but not really because I had needed to. It made me feel rather grown-up to pull the razor over my face. But now I had to shave, and to my surprise it hadn't turned out to be nearly as much fun as I had dreamed it to be.

But apart from growing up and filling out and needing to shave rather than just wanting to, it seemed that there really hadn't been that much change in me. I was still the same farm boy that I had always been. And now Willie would be cityfied and book-learned.

I thought of other changes. We had all been a lot younger in more than years when we had last seen one another— kids, still thinking that life had only good things in store for us, I guess. Willie had his dream of being a missionary, and looked like he was about to realize that dream. Camellia had high hopes of becoming someone important in the field of Interior Design; for some reason I had never been told, her dream had gone sour. She had quit and taken a somewhat mundane job.

And I was still "treading water" as far as what I was to do with my life. After I finished straightening out the farm and getting Grandpa and Uncle Charlie cared for, that is. It was taking much longer than I had first thought, but things around the farm were slowly improving.

The only problem was, Grandpa and Uncle Charlie weren't improving. Grandpa was no longer a young man. Slightly stooped, he grumbled some when he went to climb anything and he grunted when he leaned over. I knew Grandpa had neither the strength nor the desire to run the farm again.

And Uncle Charlie really worried me. Week by week it was more difficult for him to handle the household chores, things like the hot pots and peeling the vegetables. More and more Grandpa was needed to help him in the house. For now I could handle the chores and most of the farm duties myself, but what would happen after God had directed me into my life work?

It weighed heavily on my mind. But Uncle Nat had told me time and again that God would make things clear to me one step at a time. When it was time for me to pursue my life's calling, God would have someone else to care for Grandpa and Uncle Charlie.

Still, I couldn't help but speculate just how God might do that. He could arrange for hired help. But that was so costly. Unless the farm really did *much* better on the new program, I didn't see how that plan would work. He could have one of the neighbors sharecrop the farm. The Turleys were our closest neighbors, and they were really struggling after the setback of the hard winter when they lost most of their stock. They wouldn't likely be able to afford it.

Or He could direct Grandpa to sell the farm. That thought really bothered me. I knew that after having put so much time and energy into making the farm more productive, I would have a tough time watching someone else take over— especially if that someone let it go back to the way I had found it! I'd have to do a lot of praying to be able to accept the sale of the farm.

But as much as I pondered the questions about the farm, even that failed to occupy my thoughts in the days prior to December twenty-first. Most of my thinking was of my two school friends and how we would feel about each other after so many years and so many changes.

I couldn't, of course, expect Camellia to come back home and consider me her beau. I mean, I had called it all off when she didn't believe as I did. Now it would take some time and some getting reacquainted to get things back to where they had been.

I was prepared for that. In my mind I began to list all of the things that young fellas do when they court. Flowers

were hard to come by this time of year, but candy was readily
available. A fancy necklace or a bracelet might be nice. I
might even be able to find one that would match the ring I
planned to buy later on.

One thing troubled me. I didn't know how long Camellia
expected the courting to take. Would she expect me to come
calling for a number of months, or could we take a shortcut
since we had once been sorta sweethearts? I decided that I
would just have to play that part by ear.

But the wait seemed forever.

I checked out the time of that train. Three times, in fact,
I had checked just to be sure. I shaved especially carefully
that morning and shined my Sunday shoes and pressed my
shirt. Uncle Charlie had already ironed it, but he couldn't
do the job that he used to do.

After getting myself dressed I fussed and polished and
smoothed and patted and all the time I kept an eye on the
clock. I caught Grandpa and Uncle Charlie exchanging grins
and winks now and then, but I paid no mind to them.

I had intended to ride Chester; then I thought that maybe
Camellia would be anxious for a chat. We could go for a little
drive if I had the sleigh, so I harnessed up the team instead.
I threw in a warm blanket so Camellia could bundle up and
keep warm, then finally headed off for town.

I was still early, but I couldn't bear to wait another minute. Besides, I had to stop at the store to pick out a box of
candy. I had looked a couple of times before but hadn't been
able to make up my mind.

When I reached the store I tied the team and went back
to the candy counter. The girl behind the glassed-in goodies
looked at me with a friendly smile on her face. She was new
in the store, but I recognized her as one of the Tilley girls.
We had gone to school in town together but she was younger,
so I hadn't paid much attention to her. I didn't know if she
expected me to greet her now or not. I said "Howdy," but I
kept it very impersonal.

I still didn't know which candy to buy, and after trying

to sort it out in my thinking for some time I finally blurted out, "If a fella brought you candy, what would you like best?"

She smiled rather coyly and picked out a large box of assorted flavors.

"That one?"

She nodded.

"I'll take it," I said and started to count out the money.

"Could you wrap it nicely for me please?" I asked, and she nodded and went into a back room. When she returned and handed me the package, I could see she had done a good job with the wrapping. I smiled and thanked her, took the package, and left.

It wasn't far enough from the store to the station to justify driving the team. Besides, some horses spooked at the train as it whistled and chugged its way into town. I didn't want to have my mind worried with skittery horses.

I kept checking the watch that Aunt Lou and Uncle Nat had given me for my twenty-first birthday. At one point I was sure it must have stopped, but when I put it to my ear it was still ticking.

"I'll just explode if it's late," I said to myself, kicking a small pile of frozen snow near the walk. I was immediately sorry. The snow splattered all over the toe of my boot, and I had to get down and wipe it off with my handkerchief. I hoped that the handkerchief wouldn't be needed any further. It sure wouldn't do to pull it out in public all smeared up like it was now.

My impatience reminded me of the childhood game Willie had referred to in his letter, and I smiled at the memory. We loved to watch the reaction of people in trying circumstances; only we had never realized that waiting for a late train was so trying.

I had been vaguely aware that the platform was crowded, but I hadn't really looked to see if I knew anyone. In fact, I hadn't really paid much attention at all until I heard a shout, "It's coming!" and then I saw Willie's folks lined up on the platform just down from me. Most of the other folks I knew, too, at least by sight. I spotted Mary Turley and I smiled to myself. Willie might insist that they were "just friends," but didn't her presence verify my suspicions?

That's nice, I thought to myself. *Mary would make a wonderful missionary's wife. She's kind and caring, even attractive in her own way.*

The train blew its whistle then and I forgot all about the crowd of people. I forgot all about Willie's family and even Mary Turley. All I could think about was Camellia. My throat got dry and my eyes moist and my knees felt so weak I felt that I might go down in a heap.

I saw Willie first. He looked about twice as big as I had remembered him. He had on a new coat. I unreasonably thought it strange to see Willie in clothes I hadn't seen before. He looked taller and broader and much more grown-up. But his smile was the same. He yelled, "Hi, Josh!" my direction; then he saw his folks and he turned from me and wrapped his mother in his arms.

I searched over the tops of heads to watch for Camellia to appear on the train steps. I was beginning to fear something had happened and she had changed her mind. Folks seemed to have stopped coming from the train, and then Willie broke from his folks and dashed back up the steps again and when he returned he was carrying a large suitcase and an armful of parcels. Just behind, looking even more beautiful than I had remembered, was Camellia.

Her coppery hair was still wisping about her face, but in a much more grown-up style than the flowing waves of her girlhood. Her coat was a soft green color and it accented her creamy cheeks and her beautiful eyes. For a moment my breath caught in my throat, and I couldn't move or speak. Her eyes sorted through the crowd that was left; then she looked directly at me and cried, "Josh!"

Somehow I managed to get my feet going, and I moved myself forward toward Willie and Camellia. Willie grabbed me first and as we hugged one another, I remember thinking that he was likely making an awful mess of the box of candy I held in my hands.

Then he let go of me and I was standing there facing Camellia. She laughed softly and reached up to my shoulder.

"You've grown, Josh," she said in a teasing voice. I just nodded dumbly.

Then she pushed herself up on her tiptoes and with one hand on the back of my head to tip it forward, she kissed me right on the cheek. I wanted to reach out and pull her to me and kiss her again, but I couldn't move. She moved back rather quickly and looked at me again.

"I gave Willie permission to tell you the good news, but I want to fill in all the details myself. I know you've prayed for me for a long time, Josh—and I thank you. But I still need your prayers. It isn't going to be easy to see Mamma."

I nodded again. I still hadn't managed to speak a word to Camellia.

"I wrote Mamma that I was coming, but I asked her not to meet the train," Camellia went on. "I have a feeling that our meeting might be a bit emotional."

I just nodded again.

"I promised her that I would go directly to her."

I swallowed and nodded the third time. Her plans were reasonable enough.

And then she laughed again and her beautiful hair swirled as she flipped her head. "We have so much to talk about," she said. "Can you come over about three-thirty? I'm just dying to tell you everything." She stopped and looked at me again. "And to hear how things have been going with you," she concluded.

Willie and Mary were chatting excitedly beside us, but I didn't hear a word they said. I was too filled with the sight of Camellia.

I finally found my voice. "Three-thirty," I promised, then remembered the box of candy that I still held in my hand. I thrust it forward. The bow was lopsided and the paper a bit crumpled, but I guess Camellia understood.

"Welcome home," I managed.

"It's so good to be home," she said softly, and her eyes were misty with unshed tears.

Before I could say anything more, Camellia and Willie were moving away. Camellia was being greeted by his family, and I knew that she and all of her belongings would be loaded in the waiting sleigh and driven off to see her mother.

I berated myself for not having the foresight to bring the team right to the station. *I* could have been the one taking Camellia home.

But three-thirty really wasn't that long to wait. And I had some shopping to do. Now the fancy jewelry not only seemed like a good idea, but a must. I hurried off down the street to give myself plenty of time. I couldn't remember being so excited or so happy in all my life.

Chapter 16

The "Call"

It took me quite a while to find the piece of jewelry that was just right for Camellia. There wasn't a necklace or bracelet in town with a ring to match, so I had to settle for something else. I finally found a chain with a cameo so delicate that it looked like it had been made just for her. It still wasn't as pretty as the wearer would be, but nothing could hope to compete with Camellia.

I had the clerk wrap it prettily, and I carefully tucked it into the inside pocket of my coat. I didn't want to take any chances on this special package getting messed up.

I finished my shopping shortly before three-thirty; feeling generous and a bit lightheaded, I decided to go buy Sarah some peppermint patties. Pocketing the candy, I headed for Aunt Lou's.

Sarah came running to meet me. "Hi, Unca Dosh," she called, then stopped and with great concentration started over. It was obvious that someone had been schooling her. "Unca-le-J-dosh," she managed, quite proud of herself for including the proper consonants. I picked her up and kissed her, congratulating her profusely for her accomplishment. She grinned, obviously pleased with the effect of her speech.

"You come to see us?" she asked.

"No, not really. I'm going to see another—lady." I blushed even as I spoke the words.

"But you're here," she corrected me.

"Not for long. I'm going to leave again."

"Why?" she asked, looking about to cry.

"Because," I answered gleefully, and even young Sarah should have caught the excitement that I felt.

"Mamma's in the bedroom feeding my brudder," she informed me.

"Well, I didn't come to see Mamma either," I answered.

"Why?" she asked again.

"Because," I said, drawing out the small bag of peppermint patties, "because I've been to the store."

She squealed when she saw the bag, knowing it was for her.

Aunt Lou called from the bedroom, "I'll be right out, Josh."

"Don't hurry," I called back. "I can't stay. I just dropped by with something for Sarah."

"You're heading home?"

I couldn't keep the excitement from my voice. "No, I'm on my way over to Camellia's. She wanted to see her ma alone first."

Aunt Lou was silent for a minute; then her voice came back softly to me.

"I'll be praying for you, Josh."

I didn't feel that I needed much prayer at the moment. All my prayers—and my dreams—had finally been answered. With a light step I started out for Camellia's, leaving the team tied in the churchyard. There wasn't much room for hitching horses outside the boardinghouse, and in the middle of the business day I was sure all of the room would be taken. I had been to see Mrs. Foggelson several times over the years since she had taken up residence in the rambling building.

I paced myself so that it was three-thirty-one when I was let into the boardinghouse hallway, and a moment later I

was knocking on the door marked Number Four, my heart
knocking just as hard on the inside.

Camellia answered the door. She took my hand and drew
me in, exclaiming as she did so, "Mamma has just been telling me how kind you've been over the years, Josh. I will never
be able to thank you."

But Camellia was wrong. The light in her eyes was more
than enough to thank me for the little I had done.

She led me into the small, crowded room that served as
Mrs. Foggelson's parlor, sewing room, and living quarters.
It was even more crowded now, with Camellia's luggage and
packages littered about the room.

"Please excuse our mess," Camellia said with a wave of
her hand and pushed aside enough packages for me to find
room on the sofa.

"I haven't had time to put things away," she explained,
then sighed deeply. "And I have no idea where I'll find room
to put it when I do get the time." A silvery laugh followed
the words. It was so much like Camellia, so vitally alive—
and unpredictable.

She turned to me then and looked me over carefully
again. I blushed under her frank scrutiny and shifted un-
comfortably.

"Oh, Josh," she began, "it is so good to be home."

I looked at this beautiful girl-turned-woman. All the
things that I longed to be able to express died in my throat.
I could only nod and mumble something about it being good
to have her home again.

The dress she was wearing was unlike anything I had
seen before. The collar was high and shaped to highlight her
face; the bodice fitted her well-shaped waist and then flared
out in a skirt that swirled as she moved. The sleeves came
down to her wrists and tapered to a point over the back of
her hand. The color was a soft blue-green, and it accented
her hair and eyes beautifully.

"Where do we start?" she was saying. "We have so much
to catch up on."

Then she swung toward me. "Oh, my! My manners. Let me take your coat and hat."

That special gift was secreted carefully in my coat pocket. I was twirling my hat nervously in my hands. She laid them both on a chair nearby.

"Would you like some tea?" she asked.

I nodded and said that would be nice. I really didn't care for tea, but I hoped by drinking it my tongue might be loosened.

"Mamma had to deliver some sewing," Camellia informed me as she went about putting the kettle on to heat on a electric plate on a small corner table. I hadn't even thought to wonder where Mrs. Foggelson was.

"She said she wouldn't be long."

I hoped that Mrs. Foggelson didn't hurry too much.

I watched Camellia as she put the tea in the pot and tapped her trim foot impatiently, waiting for the kettle to boil. Then she poured the water, drew two plain white cups from a small shelf, and set them on the table. There was hardly room for the cups and saucers, so after Camellia had poured the tea she brought me my cup.

"So, Joshua Jones," Camellia said in a teasing voice as she settled herself on the sofa beside me, "what have you been doing with yourself in the past million years?"

She emphasized the *million*, and I found myself agreeing. In fact, the last twelve days had seemed about that long.

"Nothing, really," I answered. "Farming."

"Mamma says that you are really knowledgeable about farming. That you are trying new things and—"

Secretly I blessed Mrs. Foggelson for saying something nice about what I had been doing at the farm. I was also excited to know that the two of them had been talking about me.

"Some," I cut in modestly. "But mostly I've been just waiting—an' praying."

Camellia's teasing eyes sobered.

"I know," she said in not much more than a whisper. "And I thank you."

She sipped her tea slowly and then set her cup aside. I was surprised to see that tears had gathered in her eyes.

"I honestly don't know why you and Willie didn't give up on me long ago. I was so stubborn. So blind. I don't know why I couldn't see that you were telling me the truth all the time. That you were only interested in my good.

"Do you know what I used to think?" she said after a pause. "I used to think, 'These people are dumb. They are unlearned and they have one thing in mind only. To get me to be just as dumb and dependent as they are so that they can chalk up points for saving the most people.' That's what I actually thought. It was a long time until Willie could convince me that he was really concerned about *me*. That he knew that without God I was lost, doomed for eternity, and he cared about *me*."

Camellia twisted a coppery curl around a finger as she spoke. With all my heart I wanted to reach out and take one of those curls in my fingers but I held myself in check.

"And then this—this thing with Mamma and Papa happened. I couldn't believe it. I just couldn't bear to think of them living in two houses, many miles from one another.

"I had always been a daddy's girl. You know that. Well, I was sure that this whole thing must be Mamma's fault. I hated her. Honestly, Josh, I hated her. I couldn't understand why she had done this to Papa. I knew that she had at one time believed God. I decided if she could do that to my papa and still pretend to have known the truth—even if Papa had forbidden her to go to church—then I wanted no part of religion."

She sighed and flipped her hair back from her face.

"Well, Willie still wouldn't give up. He kept inviting me to Bible studies and to church and we had lots of talks and arguments—" She stopped and laughed as she recalled.

"Then one day I did—I'll never know why—I did agree to

go to a Bible study with him. Well, that was the beginning."
She laughed again.

"And who would have ever dreamed the end?" she said
and her eyes shone. "I was home alone in my room one night,
reading over again the portion we had read in Bible study.
It was John 5:24: 'I say unto you, He that heareth my word,
and believeth on him that sent me, hath everlasting life, and
shall not come into condemnation; but is passed from death
unto life.' Suddenly I believed it. I really believed it! Somehow I understood. I was evil, I knew that, but I could, by
believing and accepting, pass from death to life.

"I have always been afraid of death, Josh. I wanted life.
So, alone there in my room, I turned my life over to God,
thanking Him that His Son had taken my condemnation,
just as the verse said. And now I am enrolled in Willie's Bible
college instead of working at the telephone office."

"Really?" I said excitedly. "I didn't know that."

"Really! And I am learning so much, but there is so much
that I don't know. Now I wonder how in the world I could
have been so—so stupid as to believe all of those lies."

"Blinded," I corrected.

"Blinded—and stupid," she finished with a laugh.

I set my cup aside. I had wanted to hear all about Camellia's conversion, but I wanted to talk about other things,
too. If she was enrolled in college then—

"So you aren't staying home here, with your ma?" I asked.
I didn't know if I was ready to hear her reply.

"Oh no," she answered quickly. "We only have a week."

"We?"

"Willie and I."

Of course. I had forgotten that they were both going to
the same school now. They would need to be back to classes
at the same time.

"Willie should be here any minute," she said, eying the
clock impatiently.

"Willie?" I puzzled.

She looked at me with a twinkle in her eyes. "We have

something to tell you," she said. "Willie made me promise not to tell until he came."

So Willie was coming. I thought of the gift in my coat pocket. If Willie was expected soon, I'd best get some business done. I cleared my throat.

"I was wondering," I began cautiously. "I mean, well— I've missed you so much—being friends—and I was wondering, seeing you won't be here long and will need to get back to classes, if we could make the most of the days you have, sorta get to know one another again?"

It was a long enough speech for a fellow as tongue-tied as I was, but not too articulate.

"Oh, Josh!" Camellia cried, clapping her hands together. "I was hoping we could. I might have been bullheaded and mean, but I did appreciate you, and the Christian stand you took, and your prayers over the years. I was hoping—"

"How about tomorrow?" I cut in. "Would you like to go for a ride tomorrow? Maybe visit the farm?"

Her face fell.

"Oh, Josh. I'm sorry, but tomorrow I am to go to visit Willie's folks."

Willie's folks!

"Sunday?" I asked.

She made a face. "And Sunday Willie is coming here to have dinner with Mamma and me."

It seemed that a good share of Camellia's time had already been spoken for. I was a bit annoyed with Willie. He could have her company when they got back to school. Still it was understandable that he should want his folks to spend time with her. They had been praying for her, too.

"Well—" My next invitation was interrupted by a knock at the door. And I still hadn't had opportunity to give Camellia her gift.

Camellia sprang to answer the door, and just as we had both expected, Willie stood there, a big grin on his face. Camellia took his hand, much as she had taken mine, and drew him into the room.

Only she didn't drop Willie's hand. She stood there holding it and I saw Willie's fingers curling possessively around
Camellia's.

"I haven't told him," she glowed. "It was so hard, but I
kept my promise."

Willie dropped Camellia's hand, and his free arm stole
around Camellia's waist, drawing her to him.

"Josh," he said, "because you are so special to both of us,
we wanted you to be the first one to know."

I felt my throat go dry.

"Camellia and I are going to be married," beamed Willie
as a radiant Camellia reached up to place a hand lovingly
on his cheek.

I was glad I was still seated on the sofa. I knew that my
legs would never have held. The room seemed to whirl
around and around, and I was being swept along helplessly
by the tide of a dark, bottomless sea. Then, just before my
head went under, I realized that I was being watched, that
someone was waiting for an enthusiastic response from me
regarding the announcement that had just been made.

Chapter 17

Christmas

"I do believe that we took Josh totally by surprise!"

Willie's voice roused me from my stupor. I looked toward the sound and saw Willie with his arm still around Camellia, his face lit up with a broad grin.

Camellia was smiling, too. She turned to give Willie a kiss on the cheek and then moved from his arm and came toward the sofa where I was sitting.

"Isn't it wonderful?" she enthused. When I was unable to answer she continued, "Didn't you even guess?"

I shook my head slowly, still unable to express myself in words.

Willie had joined Camellia and reached out his hand toward me.

"We wanted our good friend to be the first to know—after our parents, that is. I told my folks and Camellia told her ma, but that's all. We knew that you would be—"

"Oh, Josh," cut in Camellia, "I could hardly keep our secret. If it hadn't been for you, all the years of telling me that I was wrong, all the years of praying, I might never have become a believer."

"And I would be going to the mission field all alone," Willie added rather soberly.

The spinning room was beginning to slow down. I could

hear all the words that were spoken to me, but they still seemed unreal, and I wondered momentarily if I was having a bad dream.

Willie reached down and pulled me to my feet. He thumped me on the back and squeezed my left shoulder, and the pounding seemed to start my blood flowing again.

"I want you to be my best man," he was saying.

I found my voice then. I even managed some kind of a smile. "Sure," I said. "I'd be—I'd be honored."

Willie slapped my back again. "Caught you by surprise, eh?"

I nodded. "Sure did," I was able to respond honestly. "Sure did."

And then Willie, interrupted often by Camellia, began a full account of their courtship and Willie's proposal and Camellia's acceptance. I didn't want to hear it, not a word of it—but I could hardly get up and walk out on my two best friends. I grinned—shakily, I'm sure—and nodded from time to time, and that seemed to be enough to satisfy them.

I wondered how soon they would be married, but I didn't ask. I figured that I'd find out eventually.

"And we're going to be married right here, in our little church," Willie was saying.

I did my smile-and-nod routine. Uncle Nat would have the wedding.

"I just wish we didn't need to wait," Willie went on.

"Wait?" I echoed.

"For Camellia to finish her training. I'll be done in the spring, but Camellia is just starting. She won't take four years of straight Bible courses, but she will do a couple of semesters and then go on to take classes in nursing, so that means a long wait."

I was about to ask when the wedding would take place when Camellia cut in.

"It's going to seem such a long, long time," she moaned, "but I know God can help us. Willie will put in one term on the field; then when he comes home for furlough we'll be married, and I will join him."

"How long is a term?" I found myself asking.

"Four years," groaned Camellia.

"*Four years?*" I didn't mean to say the words. They just popped out.

Willie's arm went around Camellia again. "Four years," he repeated. "A long time—but I can wait."

I didn't see anything particularly heroic about that, though I didn't say so. I would have waited four years for Camellia, too.

"Jacob waited seven years," Camellia reminded us, and Willie added quickly, "And then worked another seven."

They looked at one another and smiled. The whole scene was getting to me. I knew I had to get out of there. I pulled my watch from my pocket and studied its face. The time really didn't register, but I tried to look surprised and mumbled something about the fact that I really had to be going.

"I know you're awfully busy," said Willie, "but we have a whole week here at home. I hope we can get together often while we're here. We really would love—"

So that's the way it was. Willie and Camellia. It was no longer *me* for either of them. It was *we* now, and I was still just *me*.

"Yeah. Sure," I said. "Lots of time. We'll—we'll get together."

"That sleigh ride, Josh," cut in Camellia. "That sounds like so much fun. I hope we can work that in."

"Sure," I said. "Any time. Just let me know when it will work out."

"Hey," said Willie, pounding me on the back again as I shrugged into my coat, "I've got an idea. Why don't we ask Mary to join us? Make it a foursome? What do you think?"

Camellia was already clapping her hands. "That would be so much fun!"

"Sure," I said, trying hard to grin. "Sure—whenever you can make it."

I managed to escape then. I found my way out of the boardinghouse into the crispness of the winter afternoon. The cold air helped me get my bearings. Already the sun was hanging very low in the sky. Snow was beginning to fall in light, scattery flakes. The cold wind promised that choring would be much harder over the next few days.

But I didn't care. In fact, I welcomed the extra work. Something good and solid and demanding would help my whirling brain to sort through the news that had just been enthusiatically shared.

I still couldn't grasp it. Here I had waited and prayed for years for Camellia to become a Christian so that—so that I could feel right about asking her to be my girl. Then she finally becomes a Christian, and what happens? My friend— my best friend Willie gets there first.

I shook my head to clear it; then I realized that I was hurrying down the street in the dead of winter with my coat flapping in the breeze instead of buttoned like it should be. I fumbled with the buttons. There seemed to be a bulge in the right pocket. Then I remembered—the cameo! My special gift to Camellia. My face felt hot, even with the wind blowing cold against it. *I would have given it to her, too!* exploded through my mind. If Willie hadn't come when he did, I would have made a complete fool of myself. To think I had been dumb enough to look for a piece of jewelry with a ring to match. My face burned with humiliation.

Aunt Lou called to me as I unhitched the horses from the churchyard, but I just waved at her and shouted that I didn't have time to stop.

The horses were in a hurry to get home to a warm barn. They had been standing in the cold for too long. I let them pick their own speed and didn't even bother driving them much.

Grandpa and Uncle Charlie were both in the kitchen when I came in from settling the horses to change my clothes for choring. They seemed to look me over real good, and I was determined that I wasn't going to let anything show.

"Your friends get home?" asked Grandpa.

I nodded.

"How's Willie? Changed much?" put in Uncle Charlie.

I shrugged. "Some," I said.

"Like how?" This was Grandpa again.

"He's—he's bigger. Broader. Almost done his schooling. More grown-up, I guess."

"Grown-up," chuckled Uncle Charlie. "Never thought that Willie would actually grow up."

I defended Willie then—after all, he was my friend. "Well, he is," I said stubbornly. "He's even gonna get married."

"Willie?"

"To whom?"

"To Camellia," I stated boldly.

I hadn't wanted to say that. In fact, I hadn't even been able to admit that truth to myself yet, and now saying it out loud made me feel like I was shutting and bolting a door to a beautiful room.

"Camellia?"

"You mean, the teacher's daughter? The one that just became a Christian?"

I nodded, my eyes dropping to my boots.

I could sense Grandpa and Uncle Charlie both studying me, and then their eyes turned back to one another. I didn't even look up, just moved toward the stairs.

"I gotta change for chorin'."

I heard a chair scrape behind me and knew that Uncle Charlie was shifting his position. Then he called after me, "When?"

I didn't even turn around, just kept right on toward the stairs. "Not for four years."

I heard Uncle Charlie shift again and Grandpa give his little, "Whoo-ee," and then I heard Grandpa say plain as day, though I knew he wasn't speaking to me. "Lots of things can happen in four years." But I kept right on going up the stairs and didn't even look back.

Not until I finished with chores and supper, alone, in my

own room in my own bed, did the truth of it all really hit me. *Camellia is getting married. Getting married to Willie.* There would never, never be a chance for her to be my girl. I had no right to even think of her in that way again.

Before me flashed her beautiful face framed by coppery curls. Her eyes flashed excitedly and her cheeks dimpled into a winsome smile. I turned away from her, shutting my eyes hard to blot out the image, and I buried my face in my pillow and cried like I hadn't done since I'd been a kid.

And after I had cried myself into exhaustion, there was nothing else for me to do but pray.

For seven days I would be forced to see Willie and Camellia—together. For seven days over Christmas. There would be special parties, special services, extra outings— and I would be expected to be there. They would be there, too, arm-in-arm, smiling. There was no way to avoid them.

I thought of faking illness, but I knew that wouldn't be honest. I thought of not going, but that would get me nothing but questions to be answered. I thought of saying I was too busy, but the farm work was so completely caught up that I could hardly use that excuse. In the end I did what I knew I had to do. I went. I went to the Christmas program, the Carol singing, the party at Willie's. I even took that sleigh ride with Willie, Camellia, and Mary Turley. Somehow I managed to make it through.

We spent Christmas with Uncle Nat and Aunt Lou again. I thought about giving her the cameo, but I knew I just couldn't do that. I ended up shamefacedly taking it back, exchanging it for a brooch for Aunt Lou, cuff links for Uncle Nat and a tie bar for Uncle Charlie. That just about finished off my Christmas shopping. I added a tie and suspenders for Grandpa and then went looking for something special for Sarah and Jonathan.

I didn't call on Mrs. Foggelson on Christmas Day. I knew she was having her own Christmas that year. With Camellia home, she sure didn't need me. It was good to see the two of them doing things together. Mrs. Foggelson had even joined

Camellia in church on Christmas Sunday. It turned out to
be a good Christmas, after all. Maybe God really was answering my prayers. I was even able to think about other
things than Camellia—but that took some effort.

Before we knew it, it was time to gather at the train
station and say goodbye to Willie and Camellia. I wasn't sure
when I would see them again. Willie said that he might be
going overseas right after he finished his schooling, and Camellia planned to stay right on at the school, working in the
summer and then going back to classes in the fall again.

Mrs. Foggelson was at the station, too. She was awfully
sad to see Camellia go. They hugged one another for a long
time and cried a lot. It made me feel a bit teary too, but there
was no way that I would let it show.

Willie shook my hand, then hugged me. Camellia hugged
me too.

"You've been such a special friend, Josh," she whispered.
"I have one more thing to ask of you. Take care of Mamma.
Please. She needs someone so much."

I nodded in agreement but I couldn't help but wonder why
Camellia couldn't stay and take care of her ma herself.

And then they were gone. Several people stood around
watching the train pull out. Some of them, I imagined, would
stand right there, like they always did, until the train was
just a distant dot. I didn't. As soon as the big wheels began
to turn, pulling it forward, I turned my back on it and headed
for Chester. I didn't need to prolong the agony. I had been
through quite enough.

Chapter 18

Going On

I did a lot more growing up in the months that followed. I did more praying, too. For the first time in my life I began to realize what it really meant to turn my life—everything about it—over to God for His choosing.

As I thought about it I realized that Camellia had made the right choice. Willie was a strong Christian, intent on service for God. At first I had a difficult time picturing a woman like Camellia with her hair pulled back in a strict knot, wearing a plain dark dress and high leather boots against snakes and scorpions. Then I began to think of the real Camellia, the one that God wanted her to be—gentle, caring, compassionate—a worthy and life-enriching companion for Willie.

As I prayed and sorted through things, putting them in their proper perspective, I came to a quiet peace with the way that God was working out the situation.

I turned my attention back to the farm just in time to begin the preparations for spring planting.

I knew that we still had a long way to go in reaching maximum production, but we were on the right track. The farm looked good. The freshly painted buildings and fences glistened with each sunrise, and the fields were free of weeds and thistles—as much as we could possibly keep them. The spring calves were the best-looking bunch I had seen in my years on the farm. They looked strong and healthy, and I knew they would make good stock.

So as I entered that springtime, I began it as a more mature person, physically, emotionally and spiritually.

Grandpa seemed to pick up a bit that spring as well. He seemed to feel better, and he looked better, too. Maybe he was finally getting rested and built up after so many years of carrying the load. At any rate, he did almost as much of the farming as I did, and when I protested, he just waved it aside, saying that he never felt better in his life.

Seeing Grandpa in good form made it even harder for Uncle Charlie. He wanted so much to be as involved, but he wasn't able to do much at all.

But Sarah was allowed to pay us frequent visits, and she was good for Uncle Charlie's morale. She was going on five and quite grown-up. She spent most of her time in the kitchen with Uncle Charlie, running his errands and helping him. Being with Sarah kept his spirits up—and she was amazingly helpful, too.

A late, slow spring put everything behind for the whole growing season. Aunt Lou came out and planted the big farm garden; that saved us time and worry. And it wasn't a burden for Aunt Lou, for she loved to be involved in making things grow.

At last, some warm, dry weather arrived, and the crops took off. They seemed to sprout up overnight.

I was going through the last of the summer months thinking only of farming and a very occasional trip to the fishing hole when Grandpa caught me off guard. We were heading to town for some supplies, and I was thinking ahead, looking forward to some time with Jon and Sarah and a piece of Aunt Lou's berry pie.

"Been thinking of offering to board the schoolteacher this year."

I swung around to face him and must have given the reins

a fair jerk, for the team threw up their heads and switched their tails in protest.

"You what?" I blurted.

"The teacher," repeated Grandpa as though I hadn't heard. "I hear they need a place for her to board."

"And what would we ever do with a teacher?" I said tartly. "We can barely manage ourselves."

"That's the point," said Grandpa.

"You aren't expecting a schoolteacher to teach all day and then come home and cook supper for—"

" 'Course not! 'Course not!" said Grandpa holding up his hand and shaking his head.

"Then what did you mean? How's boarding the schoolteacher going to help us out any? And, besides, where would we put her?"

"We have extry bedrooms."

"Where?"

Grandpa looked at me like I wasn't even thinking. "Well," he said. "Iffen you recall, there is one just down the hall from you."

"*Aunt Lou's?*" I threw out the words as if Grandpa was considering treason.

"Was," corrected Grandpa. "Was Lou's. Don't recall seeing her use it for some time now."

He was being a little sarcastic, but I had it coming. Still, I couldn't imagine him letting someone else use Lou's room.

"Sarah uses it," I argued.

Grandpa thought about that for a few minutes before responding. Then he nodded his head. "I've thought on that," he said. "She does come now and then, an' I sure wouldn't want to be discouraging that." He chuckled. "Isn't she somethin'?" he went on. "You see the way she helps Charlie?"

I had seen all right. And yes, Sarah was really something.

Grandpa laughed again, an outright guffaw. "The other day she was even bossin' him. 'Uncle Charlie,' she says, 'I think you are making your biscuits too stiff. Mamma adds more milk.' " Grandpa laughed again.

"So what did Uncle Charlie say?" I asked, hoping to side-track the conversation and, thus, the ideas.

Grandpa laughed again. "He winked at me over her head and said, 'You're jest like your mamma—a little take-over.' But he loved it, I could tell."

But Grandpa wasn't ready to let his wild idea drop.

"Sarah could sleep on a cot in the corner of the kitchen," he said.

"In the kitchen? What kind of sleep would a child get there in the kitchen with you and Uncle Charlie having your coffee and talking over the affairs of the day?"

Grandpa thought about that for several moments. I had scored a point.

"You're right," he admitted at last. "I'll sleep in the kitchen."

"You?"

That idea was almost as preposterous.

"I've slept on the cot before," Grandpa informed me rather firmly.

I bit my lip. I didn't want to say something that I shouldn't.

"You still haven't listened to my full idea," Grandpa went on.

"There's *more*?" I hadn't intended to sound smart, but it sort of came out that way. I felt my face getting a bit red and knew that I wasn't fair to Grandpa.

"I'm sorry," I apologized. "Go ahead."

Grandpa cleared his throat. He seemed to feel that we were finally getting somewhere.

"You know Charlie is having a bad time getting things done around the house?"

I nodded. We all knew that. *But a teacher? A teacher would have no time and no inclination to help out three—*

But Grandpa was going on. "Well, for some time now I've been a thinkin' that what we really need is a hired girl."

A teacher? A hired girl? I didn't say it, just thought it, but Grandpa must have read my mind.

"Now, a teacher's much too busy teachin' and preparin' lessons to be able to help around the house, but to get in someone else, well that poses a problem too. Can't hardly ask a young girl to be moving into a house alone with three men, now can ya?"

I agreed, but I still couldn't follow Grandpa's line of reasoning.

I shrugged and spoke to the team. Somehow I felt hurrying them might also hurry Grandpa to his point.

"So iffen we have the teacher there; then it won't be a problem getting a hired girl," he said quickly.

"What?" Was Grandpa really proposing not one woman to live in, but *two*?

"Simple!" said Grandpa.

"And where you planning to put *her*?" I said in exasperation.

"Well, we got two spare bedrooms as I see it," Grandpa said flatly.

Gramps' room! The bedroom off the kitchen. I hadn't even thought of it—and I was surprised that Grandpa had.

I guess he read my mind again, for he kept right on talking. "A room is for use, Boy. Not for a shrine. One of the girls can have the upstairs bedroom and the other the downstairs bedroom. I don't much care who takes what. They can work that all out between themselves. Thing is, Charlie needs help, and you and I just don't have the time to spend in the kitchen. Ye ideas for better farmin' have been good, real good. But they also take lots more work to put into practice—you know that. Fella can't be two places, doin' two jobs at the same time. Now—"

But I cut in. I had better control now and spoke evenly and softly. "Have you talked to Uncle Charlie?" I felt that Uncle Charlie would be on my side.

"Not yet," said Grandpa. "Wanted to run it by you first."

Grandpa gained some ground there. It flattered me that he had chosen to confer with me. But I was still far from convinced. I thought the idea an awfully dumb one but I knew that rather than arguing with my Grandpa, I should be logical.

"What makes you think the schoolboard would okay a teacher staying with us?"

"Already talked to the board chairman," Grandpa admitted.

"And if the teacher refuses?"

"She hasn't. Says that our place is right handy to the school and that it is easier to board where there aren't lots of kids."

So this wasn't some sudden idea of Grandpa's. He had already been working—behind our backs.

"Where could we find a hired girl?" I asked next, hoping that I'd stumped him on that one. There weren't many girls in our area old enough to know how to keep house who weren't already keeping their own.

"Mary Turley," said Grandpa simply.

"Mary? Mary is needed at home."

"Not anymore. Her ma is feelin' just fine now, and she has two younger sisters who—"

I was beat on that point. I tried for another. "Who says she'd be willing to come? She—"

"She did," Grandpa said frankly.

I felt anger starting to rise. There sat Grandpa throwing out this wild and crazy scheme; he hadn't talked to either Uncle Charlie or to me before, but he had been sneaking around arranging the whole thing without us even having the chance to have our say. I had never known Grandpa to do anything so—so *backhanded* before.

"Now wait," I said, holding up a hand just as I had often seen Grandpa do. "Do you think you've been fair? I mean here you are, making all these arrangements and not even asking Uncle Charlie or me what we think about the whole business. Don't you think you should have asked our opinions? After all—"

"I'm askin' ya now," Grandpa said smoothly.

"Well, it sounds to me like it's a little late," I continued. "I mean you've decided—"

"Nothin's decided."

"But you've *asked*."

"Just put out some feelers," argued Grandpa.

"Quite a few feelers, I'd say," I countered rather hotly.

"Two," said Grandpa. "Whether we could keep the teacher as a boarder, and whether we could hire some help."

"We haven't even talked about whether we can *afford* the help," I reminded him. "What if we don't get a crop? What if—"

He surprised me by chuckling. "That's the beauty of the whole plan," he said. "The teacher's board pays the hired girl."

I could only stare. He had thought of everything.

I shrugged my shoulders helplessly. I still didn't like the idea one bit. What in the world would we do with two women in the house? We'd been alone for so long, and we knew our own routine and our own quirks. How in the world would we ever make room and allowance for two women? How could Grandpa even think that it would work?

Yet it was still his house.

Then I thought of Uncle Charlie. It was true that Uncle Charlie found it difficult to care for the household, but at least he still had the feeling of being useful. Uncle Charlie would never agree to having a woman come in and take over his kitchen. Why, that would be admitting that he was no longer of use to anyone. Uncle Charlie would never be shelved like that.

"As I see it," I said, mustering my courage, "it's Uncle Charlie's decision. The house is his area."

"Exactly!" agreed Grandpa enthusiastically. "That's just the way I see it, too."

Did Grandpa know Uncle Charlie better than I did? I slapped the reins over the rumps of the horses.

Chapter 19

Arrangements

Sarah pleaded to go with me to the store, and I couldn't resist the coaxing in her eyes.

"You know your mamma and papa don't want me to buy you candy," I warned her as I led her by the hand to the waiting team.

"I know," she said cheerily. "But I like being with you anyway, Uncle Josh."

She could say her *j's* just fine now. She could also sweet-talk. I looked down at her to read her face, but she seemed so open and honest. I gave her hand a little squeeze.

"I like being with you, too," I assured her.

"Where do we go first?" she asked me as I lifted her up onto the wagon seat.

"First the feed store, then the post office, then the hardware, and finally the grocery store."

She seemed quite satisfied with our schedule.

The feed store didn't take long; I threw the two bags of supplement feed on the wagon and we moved on.

The post office was busy, and I had to stand in line for some time before the clerk handed me our mail. But it was worth the wait. There was a letter from Willie. I tore the envelope open before I even returned to the wagon and began to scan the pages.

"What you got? A letter for you?" asked Sarah from her perch on the wagon seat. I nodded and climbed up beside her.

"Are you gonna read it?" she asked further, which I thought was rather a silly question seeing as I was already reading it. And then I realized that the questions were to remind me that Sarah was there beside me, feeling a need for a little of my attention. I reached out and took her tiny hand.

"There's a new catalog there," I told her. "Would you like to look at that while I read my letter?"

Sarah responded immediately to the arrangement.

"We'll both read our mail," she said with a grin.

The first part of Willie's letter was all about Camellia and their courtship and their plans and what a wonderful person she was and how she was learning and growing. I skimmed quickly since it was still rather painful.

Then I came to a part that really interested me. Camellia had been to call on her pa.

It was really hard for her, wrote Willie. It was easy to understand that. I knew how Mr. Foggelson felt about religion of any kind, and I could imagine how he would respond to Camellia's becoming a believer.

But as tough as it was, she was glad that she went, the letter went on. *For one thing, it helped her to understand her ma more. When we were home at Christmas Camellia tried hard to pursuade her ma to go back to her pa. Her ma just shook her head but wouldn't say anything about the situation. It made Camellia very angry with her mother.*

You can imagine how surprised Camellia was to discover that Mrs. Foggelson didn't stay behind—she was left behind. Mr. Foggelson has no intention of ever resuming the marriage. He told Camellia that her mother had written him twice asking him to forgive her for not being the kind of person she should have been, and for going back on her Christian faith. She also told him that she would be willing to try again, but that she had to be free to be the person that she had been before their marriage—that is, to be a Christian.

Camellia finally realized that Mrs. Foggelson would have joined Mr. Foggelson again, but this time she would stand firm for her Christian beliefs. Needless to say, he would not agree. In fact, he had quite made up his mind long before he moved from town. He told Camellia that he had found someone "more compatible." It nearly crushed Camellia.

For a moment I was filled with such anger toward Mr. Foggelson that I could feel my whole body tensing. Then I remembered that he was a victim of lies and deceit. His false beliefs had taken him down a dark and destructive path. Only God could reach out and open his blinded eyes.

But I felt terribly sorry for Camellia. How shattering it must be to discover the truth about the father that she had idolized for so many years.

Willie's letter went on. *What I really wanted to share is my good news. I went before the Missions committee last week and was accepted. I am to leave for South Africa in two weeks' time. Of course, I go with mixed emotions—I can hardly bear the thought of leaving Camellia behind, but she is tremendously brave about it. She—*

And Willie's letter went on and on about the virtues of his betrothed.

A tug on my sleeve reminded me that I had company. Sarah's little eyes turned wistfully to me.

"Are you done yet?" she asked, handing the catalog back to me. "I am."

I nodded. "I'm done, too," I told her. I still had so much to think about, but now wasn't the time. I would reread the letter and digest the contents.

"Now where?" asked Sarah as I lifted the reins.

"The hardware store. I need some nails, and some rivets for fixing harness."

Sarah waited patiently while I made my purchases; then we crossed the street to do the grocery shopping.

As I was depositing the parcels in the wagon, Sarah looked at me with big blue eyes. "Do you need anything at the drugstore?" she asked.

I shook my head and was about to lift her up to the wagon seat when I stopped. "Why?" I asked her.

"Just wondering," she said with a shrug of her slight shoulders.

A light began to dawn. "You know I told you I couldn't buy any candy today."

"I know," she said with a sigh, then added sweetly with a tip of her head, "but I didn't know if a soda counted or not."

"Come on, you little trickster," I laughed, taking her hand. "I don't know about a soda, but an ice cream cone might be okay."

Sarah skipped along beside me, her tiny face beaming.

"I want chocolate," she chirped. "What do you want, Uncle Josh?"

When I reached Aunt Lou's to drop off Sarah and pick up Grandpa, I heard part of a conversation that wasn't really intended for me. I was not trying to eavesdrop; I just came in quietly and at the wrong time.

Sarah had not come in with me. As we pulled into the yard we saw little Janie Cromstock from two houses down. She and Sarah were good playmates, and Janie called Sarah to come play on her new swing.

"Can I please, Uncle Josh?" she pleaded.

"You have to ask your mamma," I reminded her.

"Can you ask for me? Please?" Her big eyes searched mine. "You're going in anyway," she reminded me.

"Okay," I said, "I'll ask, but if it isn't okay with your mamma I'll call you and I'll expect you to come right home."

She nodded in agreement, and tripped off after Janie.

Thinking Jon might be taking his afternoon nap, I entered the back porch quietly and upon hearing my name hesitated a moment.

". . . does Josh think?" Aunt Lou was asking Grandpa.

"He kicked about it," Grandpa said in reply and then chuckled. "But he didn't make as much fuss as I feared he might."

"So are you going to do it?"

"Have to get it past Charlie first," said Grandpa matter-of-factly.

"And do you think he'll agree?" Again Aunt Lou was questioning.

"Just depends." Grandpa sounded thoughtful. "I know Charlie needs the help, but I also know that Charlie needs to be needed. Iffen he can give up his household duties and still feel he's not just in the way, then I think he'll agree. It all depends."

I knew then that Grandpa had talked to Aunt Lou about his crazy scheme. I was about to burst in and tell Aunt Lou what I thought of the idea when I heard her say, "It would be such a load off my mind. I worry so about you—all of you. I think that it would be the wisest thing you've ever done." Then she added quickly with a chuckle, "Since you had me, of course."

I knew better than to let my feelings be known. I hesitated, made a bit of noise with the door and tapped lightly before entering the kitchen. Grandpa and Aunt Lou were sitting at the table sipping from tall lemonade glasses. Lou looked up.

"Did you sell Sarah?" she asked playfully.

"She begged to go to Janie's to try a new swing. I said I would ask your permission. Can she?"

Aunt Lou shrugged and laughed. "I guess she already has," she responded.

"Yeah, but I told her I'd call her if it wasn't okay with you."

"It's okay. At least for a few minutes. I'll call her after she's had a while to play."

Aunt Lou rose to pour me some lemonade and pushed the oatmeal cookies toward me.

"Get everything ya needed?" asked Grandpa, and I nodded.

"Got a letter from Willie, too," I said.

"Any news?"

I turned to Aunt Lou, who had asked the question. I wasn't one for sharing gossip, but I felt that she had to know some of the information Willie's letter had contained.

"I know how you have been seeing Mrs. Foggelson and studying the Bible with her and all since she started coming back to church again. I know that you are excited about the way she is seeking to let God lead in her life again." I hesitated. "But I also know that you, like me, have been a little impatient with her for not going back to Mr. Foggelson."

Aunt Lou nodded, her big blue eyes intense.

"Well, Camellia went to see her pa and found out the truth," I said. For a minute I couldn't go on. I felt like I was about to disgrace the whole Foggelson family.

I swallowed hard. "It wasn't Mrs. Foggelson's idea to stay behind. Mr. Foggelson had found a—a 'more compatible' someone."

I heard Aunt Lou's little gasp; then her eyes brimmed with tears. "The poor soul," she whispered.

"She has never breathed one word about it," Aunt Lou continued. "It must be terribly hard for her—folks all blaming her, and all."

I nodded.

Just then Jon came toddling into the kitchen. His eyes were still bright from sleep, his cheeks rosy, his hair rumpled, and his clothes slightly damp from the warmth of his bed. He dragged a lumpy-looking discarded doll of Sarah's behind him, and when he saw us his eyes lit up and he headed straight for Grandpa.

He was met by open arms and Grandpa cuddled him close and kissed his flushed cheeks.

"Thought yer goin' to sleep the whole day away, Boy," Grandpa told him. " 'Fraid I wasn't even goin' to get to see ya."

Jon pointed at the cookie plate and then squirmed to get down. I was flattered when he ran to me as soon as his little legs hit the floor. But my ego didn't stay inflated for long. It turned out I was closer to the cookie plate than Grandpa, and as soon as I picked the little boy up, his pudgy hands were grabbing for all the cookies on the plate.

I settled him back and removed all of them except one, then pushed the plate out of reach. He lay back against me, munching on his cookie.

I held him until he was finished and then Grandpa stood.

"We best be gettin' on home, Boy," he said, studying the clock on the wall.

"Have you started the harvest yet?" asked Aunt Lou as Grandpa retrieved his stained, floppy hat.

I knew that the question was directed at me. I was the one who made the major decisions at the farm now. Grandpa and Uncle Charlie, without really saying so, had handed the reins to me.

"Not yet. Hope to get going just as soon as it dries."

"Expecting a good yield?"

"Looks good so far, if the frost just stays away."

"Suppose you'll be pretty busy for the next few weeks then," continued Aunt Lou.

"Expect to be."

"We won't be seeing much of you for a while."

"Only on Sundays."

"Maybe I can sneak out and give you a hand now and then," she continued. "Sure would be nice if you had some regular help."

I couldn't help but smile. I hoped Aunt Lou didn't think that she was being subtle. It was all too obvious what she was hinting at. It was also obvious that she was on Grandpa's side.

Chapter 20

Changes

Grandpa didn't waste much time in presenting his idea to Uncle Charlie. I had wondered just how he would go about it. I figured he'd wait until I had gone up to bed and the two of them were sitting around the kitchen table having their last cup of coffee. I even had the notion that I'd like to slip down the stairs and sit on the step to hear his presentation.

But he didn't choose to do it like that. Perhaps he knew Uncle Charlie so well he decided that if it came to pick and choose, Uncle Charlie would side with him rather than me.

At any rate, we had just finished up the chores and the supper dishes and Uncle Charlie had hung the dishpan back on the hook when Grandpa came right out with it.

"I suggested to Josh today on the way to town that it might be a good idea to get ourselves a little help."

My mouth fell open at Grandpa's directness, but it didn't seem to throw Uncle Charlie a bit. He never missed a beat, just went right on swishing the dishrag over the checkered oilcloth that covered the table.

"What kind of help?" he asked.

"Cooking. Cleaning. Help with harvest and canning."

"Anyone in mind?" asked Uncle Charlie. I was surprised when I looked at him that he had a twinkle in his eye.

"Mary Turley," said Grandpa.

"Oh," said Uncle Charlie with the same twinkle, "then I take it yer dependin' on Josh to bring in the help, not you?"

I started to say something but Grandpa cut me short. "What're you aimin' at?"

"Aimin'? Why, I ain't aimin' at anything. I thought the way you started off that *you* was aimin' to bring a wife fer someone into this here house."

"A wife?" snorted Grandpa. "Fiddlesticks! Josh can get his own wife."

"I'm glad we're all clear on that," I said with a bit of good-natured sarcasm.

"Then what did you have in mind?" asked Uncle Charlie, giving the table one final lick with the cloth.

"A hired girl," stated Grandpa.

"Oh," said Uncle Charlie. Just "Oh."

"Mary Turley says she's willin' to work out fer a spell," went on Grandpa.

"Still think my idea is a more permanent arrangement," smiled Uncle Charlie. "How long do you expect a girl like Mary Turley—an' at her age—to be available to babysit three bachelors?"

"Ain't babysittin'!" protested Grandpa. Uncle Charlie didn't even seem to notice.

"How do we pay her?" he asked, and I held my breath. Here was the craziest part of Grandpa's scheme in my way of thinking. Wait until Uncle Charlie heard the whole story!

"We board the new teacher," said Grandpa matter-of-factly.

Those words stopped even Uncle Charlie. He straightened up as far as his crippled back would allow and looked sharply at Grandpa.

I could see the questions in his eyes, but he didn't voice them. Grandpa took the opportunity to hurry on.

"We got two extry rooms here. The schoolteacher gits one, the hired girl the other. That way neither of 'em are put off 'bout living in a house with three men. Then we take the board payment from the teacher an' pay the hired girl. Works good for everyone."

Uncle Charlie snorted. I knew he had some doubts.

"Where's the flaw?" asked Grandpa a little heatedly.

I could hold back no longer. I leaned forward in my chair and laid my hands out on the table. "It's a crazy scheme. A crazy scheme," I informed Uncle Charlie. "We've got no business filling our house up with women. We've gotten along all of these years, and I see no reason why we still can't. They'll just come in here and start putting on white tablecloths and asking us to take off our work boots an' starching all the shirts an'—"

I hadn't run out of steam, but Uncle Charlie moved away from both of us. I thought that he was dismissing the whole crazy idea, but he was just hanging up the dishrag.

As he approached the table I started in again. "I know it's tough for a while at harvest, but harvest doesn't last long, and we can always get help. I'll bet we can get Mrs.—"

"I hope not," cut in Uncle Charlie. "Nearly drove me crazy, that woman."

"Then we'll get someone else. There are lots of women who cook out at harvest time. We'll—"

"Name me a few," said Grandpa. "Remember the time we had finding someone last harvest?"

It was a sobering fact. We'd had a tough time. All of the neighborhood women were busy with canning and their own threshers every fall.

"Well, we still don't need someone to live in, to stay here and change everything about our lives. We have our own way of doing things. Our own routine. We wouldn't feel like it was even our house anymore."

Uncle Charlie lowered himself slowly to a chair at the table. I could see that his back was giving him pain again.

"And where would we put them?" I went on. "The upstairs bedroom is Aunt Lou's and the downstairs one"—I waved at the door of the small room off the kitchen—"is Gramps'."

Uncle Charlie didn't seem to be listening to me and Grandpa wasn't saying much.

"We don't even know what this here new teacher will be like. She might—she might be—disgusting."

I couldn't think of anything specific to charge her with.

Uncle Charlie raised his eyebrows at that and turned his gaze toward Grandpa. Grandpa understood his unanswered question and responded.

" 'Course I checked her out. I wouldn't want her spittin' tobaccy through the cracks, now would I?"

Uncle Charlie's mustache twitched slightly, and I knew he was hiding a smile.

"She's from a good Christian home over near Edgeworth. She's got high recommendations, and hopes to become part of our church. She asked about stayin' in a Christian home when she applied here," went on Grandpa.

Still, Uncle Charlie looked a bit doubtful for a moment. He spoke for the first time for several minutes.

"Her folks would okay her staying on here?"

"We been checked out," said Grandpa frankly.

"What family would let their young girl stay with three old bachelors?" I argued. "Surely they—"

"Let's do it," said Uncle Charlie.

I couldn't believe my ears.

"What do *you* think, Josh?" Uncle Charlie surprised me by turning to me. Hadn't he been listening to a thing I'd said?

"He said it was your kitchen, and your decision," Grandpa answered on my behalf.

"Did ya?" Uncle Charlie looked squarely at me.

"Yeah, but—" I began.

"Then let's do it," Uncle Charlie said again, emphatically. "I think it's time we had a woman here in this house."

I was stunned. I couldn't believe Uncle Charlie had let Grandpa talk him into something so foolish. Then it began to dawn on me that Grandpa really said very little. I had been doing most of the talking, and I might have just talked myself right into a corner.

I was even more sure of it when I was preparing for bed and Uncle Charlie's voice drifted up the stairs to me.

"I'm worried some about Josh," he said.

"Meaning?" asked Grandpa.

"Did ya hear 'im? Sounded like he was scared of women— or else thinks thet they are a curse rather than a blessin'. Talked all thet silly stuff 'bout them messin' up his routine."

"Yer right," sighed Grandpa. "Guess Lou is the only woman Josh has really had much to do with."

"Hope we ain't too late," said Uncle Charlie and there was genuine concern in his voice.

I reached out and closed my bedroom door. Uncle Charlie's words made me angry, but I began to feel a little scared, too. Did I really feel that way about women? Was it too late? It was true that I dreaded the thought of sharing the house with two of the opposite sex. But why? I loved Aunt Lou. I loved little Sarah. I loved—or *had* loved—Camellia. What was I afraid of—fighting against?

And then it hit me. Uncle Charlie hadn't been so fond of the idea, either. I could see it in his face. But without even arguing, he suddenly said, "Let's do it." And I was the reason. Uncle Charlie might not like a woman coming in and taking over his work and putting him aside. He might even feel useless and not needed any longer, but he was willing to sacrifice the way he felt because he was worried that I was developing unhealthy attitudes.

I decided that I wouldn't say any more about the arrangements and when Grandpa asked me straight out, I told him to go ahead and do whatever he thought it wise to do. I was pretty sure what that would be.

Mary moved in first. Grandpa went over with the wagon and fetched her. She came with a small suitcase and a worn trunk, and I helped Grandpa haul it in.

I didn't feel too uncomfortable with Mary. After all, we had known one another since we were kids and she was a member of our church and all. It wasn't like a complete stranger coming into our home. Still, it was hard to adjust to having someone else around.

She chose the downstairs bedroom because she said it made more sense for her to be close by the kitchen, seeing as she would spend most of her time there.

We didn't need to worry about Mary knowing how to do household chores. She had been tending house since she had been a young girl. She moved in and took over that kitchen, yet I had to admire her—she didn't push Uncle Charlie aside. She asked this and praised that until she had him wrapped around her little finger. Didn't take long, either. And she found him more little jobs to keep him busy than I would have ever thought possible.

They worked there in the kitchen together. I could hear them chatting and chuckling each time that I came near the house. It upset me a bit at first; then I began to realize how good it was for Uncle Charlie, and I started being thankful for Mary and her sensitivity.

Special treats began to show up at the table, too—green tomato relish and fresh butter tarts and oven-baked squash. Uncle Charlie had done his best, but Mary's best was definitely better.

Mary had been there only a week when the new teacher moved in. Mary had already busied herself cleaning Aunt Lou's room until it sparkled. She even put in a small bouquet of fall flowers and a tiny basket of polished apples.

Mary may have been excited, but I was dreading the thought of sharing a house with a finicky schoolmarm. I made myself scarce the day Miss Matilda Hopkins was to arrive. I wanted to be as far away from the house as possible. It wasn't hard to do. We were already into harvest, and I had lots to keep me busy.

Miss Hopkins was to arrive by train, and Grandpa volunteered to go to the station to meet her.

I worked late. The supper hour came and went, but I purposely paid no heed to it. It was still light enough to work the field, so I just stayed working. Even though my stomach was complaining bitterly, I disregarded it. I was in no hurry to get to a kitchen overrun by women.

When it finally got too dark to see any longer, I unhitched the team and headed for the barn. I took my time watering and feeding the horses and giving them a good rubdown. A quick check around told me that Grandpa had already cared for the other chores. Normally I would have been thankful for that but tonight it just irked me a bit. I would have no excuse to escape the kitchen.

I finally headed for the house, grumpy and dirty. I knew that introductions would be in order and I also knew that I sure didn't look my best. Well, I didn't care. What difference could it make to some old-maid schoolteacher anyway?

I stomped my way across the back veranda and pulled open the door. The kitchen was empty, except for Grandpa and Uncle Charlie.

"Working kinda late," Grandpa observed.

I stared around rather dumbly, but I wasn't going to ask any questions. I crossed to the corner basin and poured myself a generous amount of water. Then I set about sloshing it thoroughly over my hands and face. When I looked up I noticed that I had also sloshed Mary's well-scrubbed floor and spic-and-span washstand. I pretended not to notice and moved toward the table.

"Where's supper?" I asked, trying to sound casual.

"Supper was over a couple hours ago," said Grandpa, not even looking up from the paper he had gotten from somewhere.

"Yours is in the warmin' oven," said Uncle Charlie around his section of the paper.

I crossed to the warming oven and found a generous serving. I hadn't realized how hungry I was until I saw and smelled the food. Even so, my good sense told me that it had been much better a couple of hours earlier. Well, that wasn't Mary's fault, I had to admit.

"Where'd you get the paper?" I asked around a mouthful.

"Matilda," said Grandpa.

"Matilda?"

Grandpa just grunted.

"You mean Miss Hopkins?"

"She wants to be called Matilda," Grandpa spoke again.

There was silence as the two men pored over their sections of paper. We didn't often see a daily paper in our house, and they seemed to find this one awfully intriguing.

"So she arrived, huh?" I tried again.

"Yep," said Uncle Charlie; then he began to read aloud to Grandpa some bit of interesting news that he found in the paper. Grandpa listened and then they read in silence again. Soon it was Grandpa's turn to read some little bit to Uncle Charlie. I expected they had been sitting there doing that all evening, and I also expected they would keep right on doing it. Some exciting evening this was going to be!

I finished my meal and pushed my plate back. "Any dessert?" I asked.

Grandpa waved a hand that still clutched the paper. "On the cupboard," he said and never even looked up.

I found fresh custard pie—my favorite—and helped myself to a large piece. That was one nice thing about having Mary around—she sure could bake a pie! I had a second piece.

The two men still hadn't stirred except to read to one another every now and then. They were really enjoying that paper.

My eyes traveled to Mary's bedroom door. It was open a crack and I could see a neatly made bed and the small desk in the corner of the room. It was clear that Mary was not at home.

Finally I could stand it no longer.

"Kind of quiet," I said. "Where is everyone?"

Grandpa lowered his paper just enough to look over it at me. "We're here," he said simply.

I blushed and ran a hand through my unruly hair. But Grandpa still didn't pay much attention to me.

Uncle Charlie folded his section of paper carefully and

laid it on the table beside him. He removed his tiny round reading glasses.

"You know," he said to Grandpa, "I think Matilda's right. A man does need to read the daily paper to keep up with what is goin' on in the world. I can't believe all the things I've learned in just one night."

Grandpa grunted his agreement and shuffled through some more paper.

I carried my empty pie plate to the cupboard and piled it with my dinner plate—more out of habit than consideration. I was about to say I was going up to bed when Grandpa looked up.

"Oh, Josh," he said, "Mary took Matilda over to her folks to introduce her. I let them hook Chester to the light buggy. Hope you don't mind."

I just stood there letting the words sink in. Not only were they taking over my kitchen and my house, but my horse as well! Anger welled up within me, but at the same time I realized how juvenile it was to feel the way I did. I calmed myself, muttered some kind of reply to Grandpa, and started to climb the stairs.

"Goin' to bed already?" Uncle Charlie called after me.

"Yeah," I replied, not even turning around. "It's been a long day."

"Sure you don't wanta read a little of the paper here?" Grandpa asked.

I was in no mood for reading Matilda's paper, I can tell you that, but I didn't say so to Grandpa. At least not in those words.

"Think I'll just go on to bed," I said instead.

But I couldn't sleep. I lay there tossing and turning and listening for the sound of buggy wheels.

They finally came. Then I could hear their whispering voices as they approached the house after putting Chester in the barn. They sounded like two young kids sneaking in the back door, but they weren't kids and they weren't sneaking in. Grandpa and Uncle Charlie were waiting right there at the kitchen table where I had left them.

I could hear the rattling of cups as Mary made them their before-bed coffee and then there was general chatter and some soft laughter and finally footsteps on the stairs, and then the house was quiet for the night.

I still couldn't go to sleep. It seemed that life was out of control. All the old familiar ways seemed to be changing. Even our familiar routines seemed to be gone.

Then I thought of Grandpa and Uncle Charlie and that last cup of coffee, and I realized that things weren't really so different after all.

Chapter 21

Harvest

I wasn't in a much better mood when I awoke the next morning. I hadn't had much sleep, but mostly I had my mind set to be ornery.

I got up early and went out to get a start on the chores. First, I went to check out Chester. I couldn't find anything to get upset about so I went on down the lane to let the cows up for milking.

It wasn't long until Grandpa joined me at the barn.

"Yer up early, Boy," he greeted me. "You musta had a good sleep last night."

I didn't make any comment.

"How's the cuttin' comin'?" Grandpa went on.

"Fine," I answered truthfully.

"Does it look as good as we hoped?"

I had a hard time keeping the excitement out of my voice. The crop was a good one. It looked like it would beat any yield we'd ever had.

I forgot my sour mood momentarily and concentrated on sharing the report of the field with Grandpa. His eyes took on a twinkle as I talked and his mustache twitched in satisfaction now and then.

By the time I had finished raving over the crop, Bossie was bellowing to be milked. We parted ways; I went on to slop the pigs and Grandpa grabbed the milk pail.

I had almost forgotten my dread of going in to breakfast and was thinking instead about the tractor I was dreaming of purchasing. I was walking toward the chicken coop with my head down when I unexpectedly bumped into something.

Now I had walked that path many, many times over the past years, and I knew very well that there shouldn't be anything in that spot one could bump into.

My head came up and my hand reached out at the same moment. And there, standing with her back to me and looking around as startled as I had been, was a slip of a girl.

"I—I'm sorry," I mumbled, pulling my hand back from her shoulder where it had landed. "I wasn't watching where—"

What's she doing standing there in the middle of the path, anyway?

She was shaking her head back and forth, the startled look giving way to mirth. "It's my fault. I shouldn't have been standing here in the way—I've been drinking in the sunrise."

Drinking in the sunrise? I had never heard it expressed like that before. My eyes shifted to the east and was astonished to realize the sunrise was worthy of such an expression. I stood staring at it—seeing it like it was the first time.

"It is pretty, isn't it?" I mumbled. "Could I help you?" I asked. "Are you looking for someone?"

She looked puzzled at my question, then began to laugh. "You must be Josh," she said, rather than answering my question.

I nodded, but I didn't see what that had to do with anything.

"I'm Matilda," she said simply, extending a small hand.

My mouth must have hung open at that. I had expected an older woman, with hair swept severely back from her face and a dark blue, long-skirted dress with lace at the throat and sleeves. But I was facing a girl who looked no more than seventeen, with bouncing, light brown curls and sparkling eyes, in an attractive dress of green calico.

"Matilda Hopkins," she said again. "The new teacher."

I still couldn't speak.

Then Matilda changed the subject completely, her enthusiasm spilling over in a candid fashion. "I love your horse, Chester. He's just bea-u-ti-ful." She stretched the word out, emphasizing each of the syllables.

"I've never seen such a beautiful horse," she went on, "and Mary says that he is saddle broken too. I'd love to ride him sometime. I'd just love to!"

She took a breath and finished more slowly, "If you wouldn't mind, that is."

I found myself shrugging my shoulders and saying "of course not," and Matilda was beaming her joy and thanking me profusely.

"But I must get in. I'll be late for school on my very first day if I keep dawdling."

And she was gone, tripping down the path in a most undignified way for a schoolteacher.

I could only stare. And then I began to laugh. What had I been so upset about? Why had I been so scared? There was absolutely nothing to fear from this child. It wouldn't be much different than having Sarah around.

I chuckled all the way to the chicken coop.

Friday night there was a Youth Group meeting at the church. Grandpa suggested, rather slyly, that I might want to break from the field work a bit early and take the girls. At first I was going to decline, and then I figured that it really wouldn't hurt. I knew Uncle Nat felt that the farm work shouldn't really come before my church commitments, so it might be wise for me to follow Grandpa's suggestion.

I should have taken the team, but I guess I just wanted to show Chester off a bit. The light buggy would be faster than the heavy wagon, but the light buggy also was very crowded for three people. It was really only made for two.

Grandpa raised an eyebrow when he saw me hitching up. I knew what he was thinking.

"Won't be a problem," I said before he could comment. "Both those girls are so small I could fit four like 'em on that seat."

Grandpa didn't say anything.

When I went in to do my last bit of slicking and polishing Uncle Charlie looked at me good-naturedly.

"Figure you might take a bit of teasin' showin' up with two girls, Josh?" he asked me.

His question caught me completely off guard.

"Girls?" I said. "One of them is Mary and the other—well, she's just a kid."

Uncle Charlie looked surprised at my assessment but he didn't say anything.

I was ready before the girls were, which was always a puzzle to me. I had put in a full day in the field, helped with chores, hooked up Chester, and still had to wait.

Mary showed first. She really did look nice, and I remembered thinking again that Willie really had missed out—until I also remembered just who Willie had ended up with.

What is taking young Matilda so long? I fidgeted mentally, and then she came down the stairs and I couldn't believe my eyes. Her hair was gathered up away from her face and her dress was much more grown-up and I suddenly realized that she wasn't a kid after all. I also realized that Uncle Charlie had been right. I might be in for some ribbing.

But it was too late to unhitch Chester and hook up the team. The girls had already expressed their delight in the light buggy. I gathered up the reins and climbed aboard. I wasn't sure how to arrange the seating.

Mary took charge.

"Why don't you sit in the middle, Josh, and one of us will sit on each side," she suggested.

I don't exactly know why I agreed, except I didn't know what else to do, so I sat down in the middle, a girl on each side of me. It was crowded, and I guess they feared they might get bounced right off the seat with Chester moving along like he always chose to do. Each grabbed an arm and hung on for dear life. I was hard put to handle the reins.

I began to sweat. I didn't know if I had the right to pray over such things or not, but I sure was tempted. I hoped there would be no fellas outside watching me arrive. But it was a warm fall night, and the fellas always stood outside and laughed and talked and watched everybody as they came.

Oh, boy, I thought, *have I gone and done it now!*

I wanted to put the blame on the girls. What did Mary go and fix herself up like that for, and why had Matilda chosen *this* night to look her age? How old was she, anyway? And why hadn't she warned me?

But I couldn't blame them. Chester and the buggy had been my idea. I'd wanted to show off my horse—and look where it had gotten me!

Mary and Matilda didn't seem to have any problem with the arrangement at all. They laughed and chatted all of the way to town, with me right there in the middle.

At one point a big jack rabbit sprang from the grass in the ditch, making Chester shy to his right. It wasn't dangerous; Chester was a well-trained horse, and it only startled him.

But it was enough to give the girls quite a scare. They grabbed hold of me with both hands. Matilda squealed and hung on for dear life. Mary was the first to recover; her face got a bit red and she released her firm grasp and mumbled some sort of apology.

Not Matilda. I think she actually enjoyed the excitement and would have been glad to repeat it again. She wasn't like any schoolteacher I'd ever had!

When we got to the church, a whole yard full of fellas were standing there waiting. I could feel my face color and knew that I was really in for it.

The girls didn't seem to notice.

"Josh!" one of the group called out. "Got your rig pretty full, don't you?" But to make matters worse, I knew I had to get the three of us down from that buggy seat. I didn't know quite how to be gentlemanly about my situation. I mean, how was I to hold Chester and assist two young women—one on each side of me—to descend in ladylike fashion?

Uncle Nat arrived to save the day. He was just coming from the parsonage to the church, and he stopped and greeted us cheerily, then took Chester's bridle and eased him in to the hitching rail. When I was able to release the reins, I excused myself and crossed in front of Mary so I could jump to the ground; then I was able to help the girls step down one at a time.

While the boys were still shuffling and gaping, Mary was calmly introducing Matilda to Uncle Nat, a job that I should have been doing.

The entire evening was pretty much what I expected. The fellas razzed me the total time. I sweated my way through the social, vowing to myself that I'd never be caught in the same predicament again.

When we were about to go Aunt Lou called me aside. "I'm so glad you brought the girls, Josh," she said. "I hope that you can do it again. Matilda seemed to fit in well with the group."

I nodded. She had, in fact, rather been the life of the party.

"And, Josh," went on Aunt Lou, lowering her voice to a whisper, "don't pay any attention to the 'pack.'" She nodded her head slightly in the direction of the boys, who had given me razzing for bringing two girls. "There's not a one of them who wouldn't give his right arm to be in your position to-night."

I looked dubiously back at my circle of friends and I began to grin. Aunt Lou was right. I walked over to the two young ladies who had shared my crowded buggy and extended an arm to each of them.

From then on things began to change at our house. My lot wasn't really so bad, after all. In fact, many would have envied my situation.

Mary was probably one of the best cooks in the whole neighborhood. What's more, she was gentle and caring and thought of many little ways to brighten the days for each one of us.

And Matilda? Well, Matilda was Matilda. She was vivacious and witty and bright—a real chatterbox, about as different from Mary as a girl could be. Each added to our household in a special way.

I wasn't chafing anymore. There were still times when our big farm kitchen seemed a bit too small and I longed for a bit more space and a little more quiet, but generally speaking we all began to adjust to one another.

And then we went full swing into harvest. All I could think about was getting that bumper crop from the field to the grain bins, and I blocked everything else momentarily from my mind.

Chapter 22

Fall

Harvest went fairly well that year. We had the usual weather set-backs, but nothing that lasted more than a few days at a time. As the weather permitted, the grain was cut and stooked; then we had to wait on the warm sun to do the final drying of the shocks.

It was my first year to drive a team on the neighborhood threshing crew. We traveled from farm to farm working the fields. A strict tally was kept of our days worked; we were allowed one day of labor, a man and his team, for every day that we put in. If I worked for eighteen days, I would be allowed three days of a six-man crew with no money changing hands. I figured that three good days would about finish our threshing, and that eighteen to twenty-four days would be the maximum of good weather needed to take care of all of the crops in our area.

It was hard work, and long days for both the teams and the men. It was especially hard when the farm being threshed was several miles from home. Most of the farms were bunched in within a radius of a few miles, but one of them was seven miles away and another was six and a half. On those days I had to leave home early to get there in time to start the day with the rest of the men, and on the same days I got home well after dark.

Some of the men took their bed rolls and bedded down in the stack of fresh straw, tying their teams to a nearby fence post. I didn't want to stay, but rather than driving a tired team the additional miles each day, I decided to tie Chester on behind my rack first trip out. Then I left the team resting and feeding and rode Chester home each night and back again in the morning. It worked well. Chester could shorten my time on the road and also get a bit of a workout. He got too frisky when he wasn't ridden frequently.

The threshing crew represented an assortment of fellas—big and small, old and young, quiet and loud—all working together for a common goal. There were usually about six of us at a time, plus Mr. Wilkes, the man who operated the threshing machine. Some of the men worked for two or three days at a time and then sent out a replacement so they could get on home and get their own crops cut and ready for threshing. I was lucky enough to have all my fields cut before I left home.

Mitch Turley and I were the youngest two on the crew. We had gone to school together back in our little one-room school—the very school where Matilda taught now. Mitch was Mary's older brother, so he kept asking me strange questions about Mary. I soon caught on that he was really fishing for information about Matilda. It seemed that Mitch had seen her once or twice and been quite impressed.

I wasn't sure I wanted to help Mitch get acquainted with Matilda. At one time he had attended Sunday school with Willie and me. At that point he never missed a Sunday, even though he hadn't had much encouragement from home at the time. But now he never went, even though Mary tried her hardest to talk him into it. I didn't offer him much information—or much hope.

The oldest member of the crew was Mr. Smith. I think that Mr. Smith had been threshing most of forever with Mr. Wilkes. In fact, his team of bays was so familiar with all of the nearby fields that I think Mr. Smith could have stayed at home and the team could have made the proper rounds—

except that they wouldn't have been much good at forking bundles!

Barkley Shaw and Joey Smith were both on the crew part time, too. Barkley and Joey were about the age of my Aunt Lou. I had never cared that much for Barkley—always considered him a show-off. But to his credit, he had settled down a lot since he had married SueAnn Corbin and become the father of four little ones.

All of the crew were neighbor folks I had known all of my growing up years. There wasn't much said around the table about world events. Mostly it was who had lumbago, and who had the best seed grain, and who was seeing whose daughter. I learned a lot just listening to the conversation.

During the time that I worked with the crew Grandpa did all of the choring. Uncle Charlie did whatever he could, and Mary did more than was expected. Even Matilda pitched in with feeding the chickens and carrying some wood.

I didn't see too much of the household during harvest. But when I got home late at night, they would all be waiting up. Matilda would sometimes be preparing her next day's lessons while Mary mended or worked on some fancy things that Uncle Charlie and Grandpa teased her about, saying it was for her hope chest. Grandpa and Uncle Charlie would often be reading the latest edition of Matilda's paper.

They'd all ask politely about my day, and Mary would quietly prepare a snack and the evening coffee for Grandpa and Uncle Charlie while Matilda told us amusing stories about the happenings at school. As soon as we finished we'd all head for bed. Some nights I was so tired I could scarcely drag myself up the creaking steps. But then I would be off again in the morning before anyone else was even up.

For eleven days we worked that way; then it was our turn for the threshing rig. I was so nervous and excited that I could hardly stand it. This was my first year to be completely in charge of the operation on our farm. I had to make all the decisions and handle all the arrangements.

We had always hired at least two women to work in the

kitchen preparing the food for the crew, but his year Mary informed me that she was sure she and Uncle Charlie would be quite able to care for things. I must have looked a bit doubtful. I remembered some of those farm homes where the food had been a little short and the unspoken disgust of the men around the table. I sure didn't want them feeling that way about us.

When Uncle Charlie sided with Mary, I decided to let them give it a try, wondering if Uncle Charlie was simply saying what he did because he hated extra women in the kitchen.

I needn't have worried. Before the three days were up Mary had established quite a name for our kitchen. Her meals were wonderful, and she also brought refreshments to the field—steaming coffee, cold milk, sandwiches, cakes and cookies. She fed the men so well, in fact, that it was a good two hours after each meal until they were really able to work well again.

The first night we went in for supper, I could see Mitch Turley straining to get a look in the kitchen window before we entered the room. At first I supposed he was looking for his sister, but I noticed that his glance slid right past Mary, who was at the stove serving up heaping bowls of corn on the cob.

Matilda appeared just then, a big white apron nearly circling her entire frame, making her look even tinier than she actually was, and I heard Mitch suck in his breath.

Mitch didn't say much at the table, but I saw him stealing glances Matilda's way. Seeing Mitch watching Matilda made me look at her a little more closely. She seemed to belong in our country kitchen, and I suppose I was getting used to her. But now I watched, and noticed that she didn't just walk, she floated around, her full-skirted dress swishing about her legs and her hair swishing about her cheeks. She served and smiled and dished out food and witty conversation, making all the men feel that they weren't quite as tired as they had been when they seated themselves at the table. Some of them even began to make funny remarks and tell ridiculous stories on one another.

Mary worked just as fast—only it didn't look that way. She moved with a quietness and grace that I hadn't noticed before. But then, I had never noticed anything about the way Mary moved. She did nothing to draw attention to herself. She had a poise—a serenity that people felt rather than saw. In fact, Mary had a way of making people feel comfortable, at home with themselves.

But Mitch never looked once at his sister—at least, not that I observed. And if Matilda knew that she was being studied, she never let on.

Mitch wore a clean, fancier shirt the next day when he came to work. Usually we wore old, patched, faded work-clothes in the fields, because the work of pitching bundles was hard on clothes as well as bodies. Sweat drenched our shirts and straw stuck to them. Wagon wheels sometimes had to be greased and horses curried. A shirt could look pretty bad by the end of the day and nobody wanted to wear a shirt that he had to worry about. But here was Mitch looking like he was heading for town or going to the school picnic.

I guess the other fellas noticed it, too, and having been young once themselves, they pretty well knew the reason for his fancying up. I saw some whispering going on and heard a few laughs, and I knew that something was up. Barkley Shaw seemed to be the instigator; maybe he hadn't settled down all that much after all.

The day was almost over and we were just finishing up the last couple of loads. I had forgotten all about my suspicions by then, so I wasn't being very cautious. Mr. Smith was the second last wagon in, with Mitch following right behind him. As the other racks were all unloaded, I sent up an extra two men to help each team driver. Barkley and Joey were standing by, awfully anxious to give a hand to Mitch. I didn't think a thing of it at the time. Just figured that they were in a hurry to get in for supper.

Smith was soon unloaded and moved his rack out of the

way for Mitch to pull up. The unloading went well, and before we knew it Mitch's rack was empty. Then Mitch went to drive his team on, when there was a thump and one back side of the wagon dropped down much lower than the other.

He halted his team and leaned over to look. To his surprise, his back wheel had come completely off. He said some questionable words, tied the lines securely over the middle post of the rack and climbed down. That was when Joey and Barkley both pressed in, seeming to be awfully concerned about Mitch's misfortune.

They talked about the wheel for a few minutes and then Barkley moved over to his rack and came back with a can.

"I got some real good wagon-wheel grease here," he offered. "Might make the wheel work back on a little easier."

Now if Mitch had known Barkley like I knew Barkley, he would have been suspicious right there. But he didn't seem to think Barkley was up to anything. He just thanked him and started to pry at that can to get it open.

"Here, use this," Barkley said, offering him a piece of metal to pry with. Mitch went to work. I could see the lid gradually coming loose as Mitch worked his way around it with the lever. Just as it opened, Barkley tripped forward over a rough bit of ground that had been there all of the time and smacked right into Mitch's extended arms. The can flew up, along with its contents, and Mitch stood blinking through a covering of dirty black oil.

"Oh, man!" exclaimed Barkley, snapping his fingers and shaking his head in fake exasperation at his mistake. "I must a' got the wrong can."

Mitch stood looking down at his fancy shirt. It was streaked and splotched with dark patches.

"Here, fella," spoke Joey in a sympathetic voice, "let me clean ya up some," and he grabbed a handful of straw and began to wipe at Mitch's chest.

At first Mitch just stood there silently and let Joey wipe away—until he saw that the straw also contained clumps of exposed soil. Every swipe that Joey took left a smeared streak of Jones's farmland behind.

By then others had gathered and were guffawing at Mitch's expense. I figured that things had gone quite far enough.

"Okay, fellas," I said as quietly, yet authoritatively, as I knew how, "let's not keep supper waiting."

Most of the men moved on then, and I turned to help Mitch get the wheel back on his wagon.

"I'll lend you a shirt when we get to the house," I promised quietly, then added as an afterthought, "It won't be fancy, but it'll be clean."

Chapter 23

Settling In

I spent several more days back on the road with the threshing crew, and then we were finally finished for another fall. As usual, after the harvest was over things settled down considerably. There still was lots to do, but we were at least allowed a decent night's sleep in between the doing. I was glad to be home instead of on the road, and I think Grandpa and Uncle Charlie were glad to have me at home, too.

As soon as the grain was portioned out—for sale, for feed, and for seed—we got out our pencils and scraps of paper and began to figure what our profits would be.

We all worked on it. Matilda was a real whizz in math and even outfigured me at times. Mary hadn't had as much book learning but she had an uncanny sense of rough calculations. More than once she surprised us at how close she came to the correct answer—in just seconds, too.

There were many reasons to be concerned with the year's profit; my primary goal was to establish whether we had made enough to be able to purchase the tractor I had my heart set on. I had discussed it with Grandpa and Uncle Charlie, and they seemed almost excited about the idea.

After a great deal of figuring and working things one way and then another to try to cover all of the possibilities, it was decided that there was money, with some left over. With the decision finally made, I could hardly contain myself.

The tractor had to be ordered for delivery and would be shipped in on an incoming freight train. While I waited, I busied myself with other things.

Matilda decided to have a school social and worked hard to talk us all into going. I really don't think that any one of us could have turned her down, but we teased along, letting her think we still hadn't made up our minds. By the time the night came she was all in a dither. It was rather a big undertaking for her first community affair. There would be games, some special music, and refreshments, and Matilda had to organize it all.

I think she was relieved to come down from her room to find us all waiting for her in the kitchen, dressed in our best and ready to go. She gave a glad little squeal and threw her arms around Grandpa's neck.

Uncle Charlie and I just looked at one another and grinned. We had known all along that we'd be going.

This time for sure there were too many of us for the light buggy, and we still didn't have snow so we couldn't take the sleigh. Taking the rather cumbersome wagon meant we had to leave early so Matilda could be there to make the final preparations. When the crowd began to arrive, we were ready.

I noticed Mitch as soon as he came in the door. He had been at our house a few times over the past weeks—to visit Mary, he said. Uncle Charlie and Grandpa would just smile and wink at that. Mary always seemed pleased to see him. I knew she was praying for him and hoping that he was ready to show some interest in church again. Tonight he was dressed all up in a brand-new suit that I figured he must have purchased with his harvest money. He looked pretty good, too. For a moment I wished I hadn't ordered that tractor. I could have done with a new suit myself.

Matilda started the evening with some "mixers" just to get folks moving about and talking to one another. Harvest had kept everyone too busy for visiting.

After spending a half hour or more playing the games, Matilda went on to her program. Several of the school children sang songs or recited pieces. Some of them were good, some not so good. But we all clapped anyway, and some of the young fellas lined up across the back of the room, whistling shrilly.

I found it awfully hard on the ears, and then I remembered times when I and my friends had done the same thing because it seemed like the thing to do. Now it just seemed loud.

The last item on the program surprised me; Matilda sang. I had no idea that she had such a voice. In fact, I could hardly believe it as I listened to her. To think such a full, melodious sound was coming out of such a little frame was almost unbelievable. I guess that others felt that way too; the room was totally quiet. Even the babies seemed to stop their restless stirring, and when it was over there was thunderous applause and more shrill whistles. People kept crying "Encore! Encore!" until finally a flushed Matilda sang us another. But she wouldn't sing a third number though, no matter how we coaxed.

When the refreshments were served, several neighborhood women gave Matilda and Mary a hand. They had all brought sandwiches and pastries from their own kitchens.

We all assured Matilda that her evening was a complete success as we bundled up against the cold and started off for home. It was a bright night with a full moon, and the horses had no trouble at all seeing where they were going.

Once again I was on the front seat driving with one girl on each side of me. Grandpa and Uncle Charlie had crawled up on the back seat and bundled themselves into heavy quilts. The cold made Uncle Charlie's arthritis act up, so Mary had made sure that we had lots of blankets along.

At first the ride was rather quiet, with only an occasional comment followed by some laughter. A shooting star caused some oohs and aahs from the girls. Mary told Matilda she had a lovely voice and begged her to sing the song again.

Matilda began to sing, softly at first, and then Mary joined in, and the beautiful sound drifted out over the moon-drenched countryside. It was a well-known hymn, and by the time they got to the second verse I could hear Grandpa humming along with them. Then he stopped humming and began to sing, and then Uncle Charlie joined in, softly, shyly.

Matilda gave me a little poke, and I sang, too—a bit hesitantly at first, and then much more bravely. Soon we were all singing, full voice. We finished the song and went on to another one and then another and another. As soon as we had completed one, someone would lead out in another.

All the way home we sang. I had never had an experience like it in all my life. Somehow in the singing we had drawn closer together against the coldness and the darkness of the world around us. It all seemed so natural, so right.

For the first time I was sorry to see our farm come into view. I could have gone on and on just driving and singing and being close to those I cared about. Just as we pulled up to the house a star fell, streaking its way downward, then burned out and was gone—and the spell was broken.

Sarah came to visit. It had been a long time since she had spent time with us at the farm, and we had missed her.

"Oh no!" said Uncle Charlie in mock horror. "What am I gonna do with *two* bosses in the kitchen?"

Mary and Sarah both laughed.

I came home from town midafternoon to find Mary and Sarah elbow-deep in flour as they rolled and cut sugar cookies. Uncle Charlie sat in his favorite chair by the window working a crossword puzzle, but every now and then he would steal a peek at the activity. I knew that he was enjoying their fun almost as much as they were.

"What would you like us to make for you, Uncle Josh?" Sarah called. Without hesitation I answered, "A tractor." It had seemed like the tractor was taking an interminable time to come.

Sarah laughed at my response but Mary gave me a sympathetic smile.

"I don't know how to make a tractor," Sarah giggled.

"That's too bad," I said shaking my head. "If you could make me one I could cancel my order."

Uncle Charlie's head lifted from the crossword.

"No word?"

I shook my head in disappointment.

"I thought you didn't need a tractor 'til spring," Sarah offered as she patched up the leg on a cookie dog.

"I don't."

"Then why are you so apatient?"

She tipped her head to the side and sucked some cookie dough off a finger as she waited for my answer. I waited too. I wasn't sure how to answer her. At last I had to smile.

"I'm 'apatient,' " I said honestly, borrowing her word, "because I *want* it so much, not because I need it so much."

"Oh!" nodded Sarah. She could understand that.

She thought for a moment and then her face brightened. "Then I know," she said matter-of-factly. "Pray. Pray an' ask Jesus to help you wait. Before I had my birthday one time I was apatient an' Mamma told me to pray, an' I did, an' Jesus helped me wait."

It sounded so simple. Maybe it was simple. I ran a hand over Sarah's curly head. "Maybe I'll do that," I said huskily.

She seemed perfectly satisfied that the matter had been taken care of and could be dropped.

"Would you like a horse?" she asked.

"I've already got a horse," I informed her.

She giggled again. "Well, this one don't need hay, or oats, or anything," and she handed me a slightly damaged horse with crooked legs.

I ate the horse in two bites.

"Mamma don't let me do that," said Sarah seriously, her eyes big. "She says I might choke and throw up."

I wanted to tell Sarah that such talk wasn't very ladylike

and then I was reminded by a little glance from Mary that I had provoked the whole thing.

"I shouldn't have done it, either," I admitted. "I promise not to do it again."

I gave Sarah another pat, grinned sheepishly at Mary and went on up to my room.

The question of where Sarah should sleep at our house hadn't really been solved. I offered to sleep on the cot, but Grandpa refused. He didn't say so, but I think it had something to do with him having gotten two boarders for our extra bedrooms. Uncle Charlie said he would, but it was hard enough for him to get a decent night's sleep in his own bed.

Grandpa ended up on the cot that first night. He looked awfully tired the next morning.

We talked again about letting Sarah take the cot. The idea didn't seem like a good one—not that the cot wouldn't fit Sarah better than it had Grandpa, but simply because she would be kept awake so late. Sarah would never go to sleep as long as there was stirring in the kitchen, yet none of the rest of us were ready for bed at seven-thirty.

Mary finally worked it all out. "Move the cot into my room," she suggested. "There's plenty of room; Sarah can go to bed at the proper time and the rest of us can keep our own beds."

"That's awfully kind of you, Mary," Grandpa started to protest, "but you shouldn't have—"

"Nonsense," she said. "I love her company and you know it."

So the cot was moved into Mary's room and Sarah was tucked in for the night. It was a much better arrangement. After Sarah had returned home the next day, I offered to move the cot out, but Mary wouldn't hear of it.

"Just leave it there," she said. "It's not in my way, and it will be all ready for the next time she comes."

The snow came softly at first, then heavier and heavier

until there was a deep ground cover. I didn't like the idea of tiny Matilda heading off for school across the open field. It was already knee deep and there would be no path.

"Take Chester," I urged her.

"I'll be fine," she insisted. "A little snow won't hurt me. The walk does me good. Besides, there'll be worse storms before the winter is over. I might as well get used to it."

I stopped arguing, but I will admit I cast a glance out the window now and then until she passed out of sight, just to be sure that she would make it to the schoolhouse.

Storm followed storm, and we settled into another winter. Soon we all had adjusted to it, and I no longer fretted when Matilda left for school, her high boots clearing a way through the drifts and her arms full of textbooks.

Shortly before Christmas the tractor finally arrived. The station master sent word out to us with one of our neigbors. Mr. Smith seemed to be quite pleased to have been chosen to bear the news. There weren't too many tractors in our part.

I rushed off to town to pick it up and it looked like the whole town was there to watch me take delivery.

I had thought from reading the manuals that a tractor would be easy enough to handle. But we had a real time getting it fired up, and by the time the blacksmith came to give me a hand, my face was red and my fuse short.

Then I had to back the big monster up in order to get it turned around. That seemed to be harder than backing a horse and buggy. We had to start it twice more, because I kept killing the engine. I finally did get it heading the right direction, with all eyes of the townsfolk upon me. But then, not wanting to hog all the road, I got a little too close to the edge of the roadway. Those big steel wheels just seemed to pull me right on down into the ditch, and the tractor stalled again. When the helpful blacksmith and I did get it started, I wasn't sure how I was going to get myself out of there. But to my amazement, those same steel wheels that took me down so unexpectedly also took me back out, and I was off down the road heading home.

It was a cold ride. The thing moved along at a crawl, and it was made all of steel, so there was nothing warm about it—at least not back where I was sitting.

By the time I got it home, I sure was glad to pull it up beside the granary and climb on down. It wasn't nearly as easy to handle as a team, I can tell you that, and it took me most of the afternoon to get the chill out of my bones.

I did some thinking about that tractor that I hadn't done before. Getting the tractor was fine, but I hadn't thought much of where to go from there. I could tell just by looking that the farm machinery we had used behind the horses wouldn't work behind that tractor. We'd probably need to replace nearly all the equipment we owned.

I wrote Willie a long letter that night, the first one in a while. I'd had a few letters from him, and I knew he was just as busy there in South Africa as I was back home.

He was pretty excited about his new life. Oh, he still missed Camellia terribly—and his family and friends, too, I guess, but he sure was excited about getting into the work he had been trained to do. God had given him a deep love for the black Africans he was reaching out to. They were so friendly and open, he said, and he knew he was going to love being a missionary among them.

I had already told him about Grandpa's wild idea of moving two women into our house. I had even written later, admitting that it really wasn't as bad as I had expected. But I hadn't told him about the community social or our good harvest or the new tractor.

I told him, too, that Mrs. Foggelson was really doing well since she had reestablished her faith. Not that she was running around town preaching or singing on the street corner or anything like that, but she was growing in a quiet, maturing way.

I miss you, Willie, I wrote, *and I'll be glad to see you again. Four years, after all, is a long, long time. God's blessing on your work; my warmest regards. Your best friend, Josh.*

Chapter 24

Winter Ills

Another Christmas was approaching. We all went together to the school Christmas program. Matilda had labored long and hard over it. The youngsters performed well, and the crowd of neighbors insisted that Matilda sing again. She sang two lovely songs and then she asked Mary to join her for one. Mary did, without protest, and the people clapped even more enthusiastically after the duet.

The program at the church on Sunday night was mostly Aunt Lou's responsibility, though she had help from Matilda as well.

Little Sarah sang her first solo, "Away in a Manger." She was doing fine, too, carrying the tune just perfectly until Jon jumped down from the bench beside Mrs. Lewis, who was supposed to be looking after him, and ran to get in on his sister's act.

Aunt Lou didn't know what to do. To dash after Jon would interrupt the song, but leaving him alone proved to be even more disruptive.

At first he merely stood beside Sarah, looking up in her face and rocking gently back and forth to the music. Then he decided to sing, too, but Jon didn't know the words. His song was "Ah-ah-ah" at the top of his healthy lungs. Sarah frowned at him, but went on singing. It wasn't long until

Jon's "Ah-ahs" were drowning out Sarah's voice. She finally stopped mid-phrase.

"Go to Mrs. Lewis!" she hissed loudly at her brother.

He shook his head and started to sing again.

"Then go to Mamma," Sarah insisted, giving him a push.

Jon still refused to budge. I could hear some snickers and caught a glimpse of Uncle Nat heading for the platform, but Sarah hadn't seen him. "Go!" she insisted and gave Jon another push, a bit more forcefully.

"No!" hollered Jon. "Sing!" As he whirled around to escape his sister, he entangled himself in the decorated tree. It came down with a crash and Jon, frightened by it all, began to bellow as loudly as he could. By the time Uncle Nat arrived, his two offspring were both crying and the platform was a mess.

"Preacher's young'uns!" Uncle Nat said to the amused congregation, rolling his eyes heavenward half in jest and half in exasperation, and scooped up his two errant family members while Aunt Lou tried to restore some order to the front of the church.

On Monday we took Matilda to the train; she was to spend her holidays at home. She was in a dither about seeing her family again, but that was normal—Matilda lived life in an air of excitement. She and Mary had become very close friends, and they hugged one another over and over. In fact, the only one who didn't get a hug was me. I would have been embarrassed about it if I had. Us being right out in the eyes of people and all. I knew that few would understand how it was at our house. The house seemed a bit quiet when we returned. Mary served us a tasty dinner, washed up the dishes and then went to her room. Soon she reappeared with her small carpetbag in her hand.

"Your Grandpa has given me Christmas week off. With Matilda gone he says you can get along just fine by yourselves."

I was a little doubtful. We hadn't been doing much cooking for ourselves lately, and it would be rather hard now to fit back into the old rut.

"I've done extra baking," went on Mary. "You'll find it in the pantry."

I nodded.

"If you should need me—"

"We'll be fine. Just fine," I assured her with more confidence than I felt.

She pulled on her heavy coat, and I finally realized it was cold out, and it was over a mile to the Turleys'.

"I'll get Chester and give you a ride home," I offered.

I didn't wait for her to answer, just grabbed my coat and cap and headed for the barn.

I hooked Chester to the one-horse sleigh, and we set off. The afternoon was crisp and bright and the snow crunched under the runners.

"I'll miss Matilda," sighed Mary after a long silence.

I was on the verge of saying that I would too but checked myself just in time.

"She's so—so alive," went on Mary.

That was the truth. I was reining in Chester—as usual, he wanted to run.

"It won't be long till she's back."

"Oh, I hope not!" Mary gave a deep sigh.

I didn't go in when we reached the Turleys', though Mary asked me to. "I've got to get home and start in on the chores," I told her. Then I added, feeling suddenly shy, "We'll see you in a few days. Have a real good Christmas."

She turned to me. There were no rows of eyes watching.

"Thank you, Josh," she whispered. Then she reached up, gave me a quick embrace, and she was gone.

It turned out that we did need Mary. Two days after Christmas Uncle Charlie became ill. We could have handled that, but the next day Grandpa, too, was down. I didn't know what to do. I still had all the chores, and the two men were sick enough that they needed someone to care for them. In desperation I finally saddled Chester and headed back for Mary.

Mary flushed a bit when she saw Chester, but she laughed, too. "Well," she said, "does he ride double?"

"How stupid of me!" I blushed. "I should have brought the sleigh. He can carry two, but—"

"It's fine, Josh," she assured me. "If Chester doesn't mind, I don't."

She rode behind me, her arms around my waist as though it was the most natural thing in the world.

In the next few days, Uncle Charlie worsened, and though Mary nursed him with all of her skill and prepared him broths and chicken soup, he still couldn't keep anything on his stomach. I saddled Chester up again and went after Doc.

After a few days on the medicine that Doc left, Uncle Charlie seemed to be able to make some headway. But by the time Grandpa and Uncle Charlie were beginning to show a bit of improvement, Matilda was back, and Christmas was over.

Things seemed to be fine for about two days, and then Matilda came down with chills and fever. School was cancelled until further notice, and Mary started her nursing again.

When it finally hit me, I couldn't believe that anyone could feel that bad. My whole body ached, and I broke out in sweats and then shivered until the bed shook. The mere thought of food was unbearable, and I was so weak that I could hardly turn my head on the pillow.

I don't know how Mary made it through those days. She did send for Mitch to do the choring, but even so, I don't think she got much rest day or night. Whenever I stirred restlessly, cool cloths were pressed against my fevered forehead and sips of water held to my chapped lips.

I drifted in and out of reality. Sometimes I had strange dreams where I was in heaven and the angels were flitting about me, brushing back my hair and cooling my face. Sometimes I was quite rational and Mary or Matilda would be there sponging off my face or back and chest. I think that Doc was there once or twice. I don't remember seeing him; I just remember his voice giving somebody instructions.

I had no idea how many days were passing by. I only knew that when I was finally aware enough to ask, I couldn't believe that so much of the month of January was already spent. From then on I had almost constant company. Mary came with broths and soups and Pixie lay at the foot of the bed. Uncle Charlie just sat there quietly and cleared his throat now and then. Matilda came with books and read to me for what seemed hour after hour in a voice filled with energy and excitement.

By the time I was able to sit up for short periods in the kitchen, Grandpa and Uncle Charlie were almost as good as new, and Matilda had been back to her classes for a couple of weeks.

I had never been that sick before in my whole life. And after those days in bed, helpless and sick and flat on my back, I was ready to admit one thing—I was glad there were women in the house.

It turned out that Mitch had to do our chores for the whole month of January and half of February. I maintained that I was well enough to get back to work, but Doc wouldn't hear of it. My recuperation time did give me a good chance to get back into some books. I had been so busy using my muscles that I had almost forgotten how to use my brain.

I discovered, too, that the daily papers that arrived for Matilda to the post office weekly weren't all that bad. To relieve the boredom, I began to sort through them and found some terrific articles under "Farm News and Markets."

There was so much more to farming than mere sowing and reaping. I could see the possibility of the farm turning a tidy profit in the future, and the thought filled me with energy and excitement. Folks like Willie needed support in order to stay on the mission field. I didn't say anything to the family yet, but I did do some talking to God. I was beginning to get a vision of the farm being used in God's work by helping meet the financial needs of missionaries—especially Willie. I intended to do all I could to make the farm produce so that he would never need to worry about support while he served on the field.

Chapter 25

Chester

I was sitting at the table talking to Matilda about some strange ideas, to my way of thinking, I'd found in one of her books. I heard a commotion and went to the kitchen window to look out toward the barn.

I smiled. There was nothing to be concerned about. The horses were just frisking about. I looked at the sky, thinking that another storm must be moving in.

"Why are they running?" Matilda asked at my elbow.

"Just feeling frisky," I answered. "Or could be a storm coming in. Horses often run and play before a storm." We stood there to watch them for a minute.

Chester was really worked up. He loved to run, and any excuse for him was a good enough one.

Mary crowded in on the other side of me, her face lightened by a smile. "I love to watch them."

The three of us stood there watching the horses rear and kick and race around the barnyard.

"He is so beautiful!" exclaimed Matilda. She held Pixie in her arms, gently scratching under one of the dog's silky ears. But I knew that it wasn't Pixie that she referred to. It was Chester, showing off out in the barnyard. "Look at him, his head thrown back, his tail outstretched—" The word ended in a gasp.

Chester, who had been doing a tight circle around the end of the barn at almost full speed, had suddenly gone down, apparently hitting a patch of ice under the snow where the eaves dripped in milder weather.

I didn't even wait to comment; just turned and ran from the house. I guess I knew I should have stopped for my coat, especially since I had just been sick, but I didn't.

As I raced toward the barn, Chester was still floundering in the snow, pulling himself up, then tossing back down. His feet were thrashing, the snow flying, and as I ran I kept wondering why he wasn't back up on his feet.

I was almost to him when, with a snort and a flurry, he righted himself. I took a deep, relieved breath—and then I saw it. Chester's right front leg wobbled at an awkward angle. He had broken a leg in the fall!

I skidded to a halt and whirled around with my back to the horse. My arm came up and I buried my head against the fence, not wanting to see. Dry sobs wrenched my throat; then someone was gently nudging me. "Here put this on." It was Mary, helping me into my coat.

Then she, too, looked at Chester and I could hear her soft gasp.

I'm not sure when Matilda joined us. She came scurrying up beside us, her breath preceding her in little shivery clouds.

"Is he okay?" she gasped out.

Chester attempted to move, and I heard his pain-filled cry and Matilda's answering scream.

"No! No!" she kept saying over and over. I put my arms around her. She clung to me, sobbing convulsively.

When Grandpa came, we were all still standing in a huddle trying to comfort one another.

"Hurt bad?" I heard Grandpa ask.

I muttered in answer, "His front leg."

This brought a fresh burst of tears from Matilda. "I can't bear it!" she cried. "I can't bear to see him like that!"

I cast another glance toward Chester. He hadn't taken

another step. He stood there, shaking his head and snorting, totally confused by the pain.

Somehow I got control of myself. "Here," I said to Mary. "Take Matilda to the house."

Mary led Matilda, still crying, away.

For the first time I took a good look at Chester. His heaving body was still covered with snow. He trembled with each breath he drew and his leg just dangled there, supporting none of his heavy frame.

I moved toward him and reached out a hand to run down his smooth neck. He quivered at my touch, then tried to take a step. His whole body reacted to the pain, and I thought for one awful minute that he was going to go down again. Sick at the sight, I turned from him, and wretched. The illness I had just come through probably had something to do with it. But I had to get control of myself. I had to help Chester.

Grandpa hardly knew whether to go to Chester or to me. I nodded at him that I was okay and he moved toward the horse. He spoke to him in soft tones, rubbing his neck and trying to calm him, his hand moving gently down toward the injured limb.

Chester threw himself back, and the pain of the movement made him squeal again in anguish.

I whirled and headed for the house. I didn't go to the kitchen, just to the back porch, and stopped there only long enough to check that there were shells in Grandpa's big old Winchester. I was turning to leave again when I heard the door open and close. Quick footsteps dashed after me and I could feel a hand on my arm.

"No!"

I jerked my arm free and tried to keep on walking.

"Josh, listen!" But I still didn't stop. Just as I reached the door Mary pushed herself ahead of me. She stood there, her back against the door, her slight frame heaving. She had been crying, too; the traces of tears were still on her cheeks.

She stood there, defying me, shaking her head and blocking my way.

"Don't!" she pleaded again.

I reached out a hand and pushed at her. "Do you think I want to do this?" I almost screamed.

We both knew the answer.

"Then don't," she said again, not budging from the spot she guarded.

"He's suffering!" I cried. "Can't you see that? He's suffering!"

Mary reached out and placed a hand on my coat front. Her eyes looked wide with fright and determination. "Yes," she said and her voice rose to almost the pitch that mine had been. "Yes, he's suffering. But life is full of suffering, Josh. You've suffered. I've suffered." She took another deep breath and her whole body heaved. "For years—for years I watched my mother suffer—day after day—week after week. I loved her, Josh. I loved her. But I didn't give up. I fought. I fought to save her. Chester is a fighter, Josh. A thoroughbred and a fighter. Chester isn't done yet. He hasn't given up. And we can't either—not without a fight."

With her final outburst, Mary took the gun from my unresisting hands and moved away from the door. I heard the sound of metal on metal as she hung it back on the pegs. The world was whirling around me and I was afraid I was going to be sick again.

Mary brushed past me and went out the door.

It was several minutes until I got myself under control. When I could think straight again, I thought of Mary's plea to fight for Chester's life. It would never work. Chester's leg was broken; anyone could see that. There was no way we could save him now. If we tried, he would suffer and suffer and then we would need to destroy him anyway. Better to relieve his suffering now.

I looked back at the gun and then let my shoulders droop in resignation as I turned my back on it and headed for the barn.

Somehow Mary and Grandpa had managed to get Chester

into his stall. They were talking in quiet tones as I entered the barn.

" . . . a good clean break," Grandpa was saying. "No protruding bone."

"We need to keep his weight off it," Mary replied, beginning to gentle Chester with her hands and voice.

"How?" It was only one word from Grandpa, but it spoke for both of us.

"We need to construct some kind of sling—to hold him up, off his feet."

Grandpa eyed the stall. It wouldn't be easy.

"I saw Pa do it once with a critter," went on Mary. "Worked it on a pulley system."

Grandpa chewed on a corner of his mustache as he thought deeply. "Might work," he said at length.

"You keep him warm and try to quiet him, and I'll go get Pa," said Mary. I wasn't sure if she was talking to Grandpa or to me.

It was an awfully long time until Mr. Turley got there. Mary didn't come with him to the barn, but went right on to the house. I had spent the time soothing Chester. We had thrown a heavy horse blanket over him and rubbed his body down with clean straw. He was quieter. The fright seemed to have left him. He still quivered every now and then and snorted loudly when he tried to shift his weight.

Mary's pa went right to work. He called out orders so quickly that I was running to keep up. In a couple of hours we had Chester fitted with a body sling, and then with the pulley system Mr. Turley had rigged up above him, we gently hoisted him until his three feet just barely touched the floor. Chester's right front leg was raised just a shade higher so that he couldn't put any weight on it at all.

Chester, of course, didn't understand the arrangement. He snorted and pitched, trying to get proper control of his circumstances. It was some time until we were able to quiet him, and by then I was just sure it wasn't going to work.

As soon as Chester was settled down, Mr. Turley began

to work on the leg. It had swollen a good deal, so it was difficult for him to feel the break. And any pressure on the area sent Chester flailing again.

At length Mr. Turley stood up. "A real shame!" he said soberly. "Such a beautiful horse."

I thought he was going to agree with my first response, to say that nothing could be done for Chester—but he didn't.

"Good clean break," he said instead. "Should heal nicely, barring any unforeseen complications."

The breath I had been holding came out slowly.

Then with the help of Grandpa and me, Mr. Turley got a leg support on Chester. By the time we were through, we were all worn out.

Grandpa invited Mr. Turley up to the house for a cup of coffee and I slumped down in the straw, my back to the manger and one hand on Chester. I just sat there—wondering, praying, hoping with all my heart that this beautiful animal would be all right.

I didn't even hear the door open.

"Josh?" It was Mary. She spoke in a whisper. "Josh?"

The barn lantern flickered with the slight movement of air from the door, the wavering flame sending the shivers of light dancing cross Mary's face. She stood there, holding out to me a steaming mug of chicken soup. I took it in still-trembling hands.

Then without another word she lowered herself to the straw beside me and laid a hand on my arm.

"He's gonna be okay," she whispered. "He's gonna be fine."

I tried a weak smile.

"How's Matilda?" I asked, wanting to forget just for a moment the pain of Chester.

"She's okay now. She's making dessert for supper. She's been praying—steady—ever since it happened."

I sighed and turned back to Chester.

"You really think he'll be all right?" I asked Mary.

Her smile was a little wobbly.

"Look at him," she said rather than making me any promises. "Pa says his leg felt real good. The bone seems straight—it's just a matter of time."

I looked at Chester. He was much calmer now. I almost believed what Mary was saying to me.

I turned to her. "Thanks," I said, taking her hand. "Thanks."

I should have said a lot more. Thanks for stopping me from doing something foolish. Thanks for riding old Maude through the cold and snow for your pa. Thanks for bringing me the hot soup. Thanks for your support. But all that I could say was "thanks."

She gave my hand a slight squeeze, rose to her feet, and returned to the kitchen.

Chapter 26

Willie

Chester adapted remarkably well to his body harness. Maybe he enjoyed the extra attention. I spent a great deal of time in the barn with him, and Matilda visited him often with treats of apples and sugar lumps. Mary inspected his entire body at least once a day, watching for any sores that might result from the harness straps.

The swelling began to go down in the leg, and after Mr. Turley had taken a look at it a few times, he suggested putting on a new leg brace. Chester hardly complained at all as it was done.

After a few weeks the brace was taken off altogether, but Chester was still not allowed to put his weight on it. I began to massage and exercise it. I wanted to be sure that the knee and ankle would still work well. Chester was able to move it with no problem—with my help, of course.

Finally the day came when we lowered the hammock and let him test his weight. He seemed reluctant at first and snorted his concern. I rubbed his neck and spoke to him 'til he calmed down.

We didn't leave him on all four legs for long. We didn't want to tire him. But every day he was allowed to stand for a longer period of time.

At last I began walking him. At first he had a bit of a

limp, and then even that disappeared. It was almost too good to be true, but it looked like Chester was going to be just fine.

As the winter wore on, we all went about our daily chores. I fired up our new tractor every once in a while, just to make sure it was still working. Then Grandpa had the bright idea of dragging a log behind it to clear snow on our road. Uncle Charlie got in a bit of teasing about my "new toy."

We spent the evenings together in the big farmhouse kitchen, Pixie curled up contentedly on the lap of one or another. Those evening were special times. On such nights, we were comforted by the thought of being snuggled in the kitchen, a warm fire crackling in the big cookstove. We could often hear another storm as it swept through, the wind howling and raging and rattling the loose tin on the corner of the eaves trough. Every time I listened to it, I reminded myself to fix it come the first nice day. But when the nice days came, I was always busy with something else.

Every time I went to town—and I didn't go any more often than absolutely necessary on those cold days—I picked up another bundle of Matilda's papers to help pass the boredom of the winter days. It had been several weeks since I had heard from Willie, and I had been watching for a letter from him—but the letter didn't come.

Then one day I heard the farm dog bark a greeting, and I looked out the frosted window to see Uncle Nat flip the reins of Dobbin over the gate post. He came toward the house in long, quick strides, and I wondered if he was cold or just in a hurry.

I met him at the door with enthusiasm. It had been a while since he had been out.

Mary pushed the coffeepot forward and added fuel to the fire so that Uncle Nat could warm himself a bit, and Grandpa and Uncle Charlie pulled up chairs to the table, getting ready for a good visit.

Uncle Nat sat down and indicated the chair next to him.

I pulled it up and leaned forward, eager to hear how things were going in town.

"How's Chester?" asked Uncle Nat.

I beamed. "He's doing fine. I can't believe it. You should see him. He can move around almost as good as before."

Uncle Nat smiled and nodded his head.

"How're Lou and the kids?" asked Grandpa for all of us.

"Busy," laughed Uncle Nat. "Real busy. That Jonathan! Lou hardly knows how to keep him occupied in this cold weather."

We all laughed, knowing enough about active Jon to feel a bit sorry for Aunt Lou.

"You out callin'?" Grandpa asked.

"No," said Uncle Nat slowly. His head lowered and his face sobered. We all waited, knowing instinctively that there was more. He lifted his head again and looked directly at me.

"I'm afraid I have some bad news," he said. "I thought you should know. It's Willie."

"Willie?"

"He's gone, Josh."

I didn't understand.

"Gone? Gone where?"

"Word came to the Corbins by telegram this morning. Willie died a couple of days ago."

"But there must be some mistake!" I hardly recognized my own voice, hoarse with shock. "Willie is in South Africa. How do they know—?"

"The Mission Society sent the telegram."

"But there must be some mistake," I repeated, not wanting to accept or believe what I had just been told. I started to get up from my chair. Uncle Nat put a hand on my shoulder and eased me back down.

"There's no mistake, Josh," he sorrowfully assured me. "The Mission Board sent their deepest regrets. Willie is dead."

I heard someone crying, and then I realized that it was

me. I buried my head in my arms and cried until the sobs shook my whole body.

"Not Willie!" my voice was saying over and over. "Dear God, please, not Willie."

And all the time a part of my brain kept saying, *It's all a mistake. You'll see. They'll soon discover that they were wrong. It was someone else—not Willie.*

In the background I could hear voices, but the words never really registered. Someone was comforting a weeping Mary. Someone was trying to comfort me.

It was a long time until I was able to get some measure of control. Grandpa was asking more questions.

"How did it happen?"

"Some kind of fever—malaria, they expect."

"Was he sick for long?"

"They still don't know."

"How are his folks?"

"Taking it hard."

It seemed so unreal, senseless. Willie had hardly arrived out there, and now he was *gone*.

And then I thought of Camellia. And I began to cry again. "Poor Camellia. Poor Camellia," I muttered over and over.

That storm passed, too, and I sat, head bowed, shuddering and hiccuping as I wiped my eyes and blew my nose on the handkerchief I found in my hands.

"Would you like to go to your room?" Uncle Nat asked, and I must have nodded. Uncle Nat helped me up the stairs and to my bed. I threw myself down there and began to weep again, but it seemed so useless. I started to pray instead. For Willie—though I don't know why. Willie was safe enough. For the Corbins; I knew the whole family would be devastated. I had to go to the Corbins. I had to let them know that I too shared their suffering over the news of Willie's untimely death.

I prayed for Mrs. Foggelson; Willie was to have been her son-in-law. But mostly I prayed for Camellia. How would she ever bear it? She was all alone at the college, preparing herself to serve with Willie in his Africa.

She would come home now, broken perhaps, but she would come home.

I went back to the kitchen and splashed water on my swollen face. Uncle Nat had already left, but Grandpa and Uncle Charlie sat silently at the kitchen table. Untouched cups of cold coffee sat before them. They looked at me without saying a word. Mary was nowhere to be seen, but her bedroom door was closed tightly.

"I'm going to the Corbins," I said quietly, and Grandpa nodded.

I wasn't sure Chester's leg was well enough, so I put a bridle on old Maude.

I didn't bother with the saddle; just grabbed up the reins and rode bareback. Maude wasn't the easiest horse in the world to ride, but maybe I took some satisfaction in my discomfort.

I found the Corbin family tear-stained and desolate. Mrs. Corbin sat in a rocker by the kitchen stove, saying over and over as she rocked, "My poor boy. My poor boy. My poor Willie." When she saw me she held out her arms and I went to her. She held me so tightly that I could scarcely breathe, and I knew she was trying to hold on to a little part of Willie.

Mr. Corbin paced back and forth across the kitchen floor, his face hard and his hands twisting together. Other family members huddled in little groups here and there, whispering and crying by turn.

And then a very strange thing happened. SueAnn, who had been crying just like the rest of them, wiped away her tears, took a deep breath and managed a weak smile.

"I know God doesn't make mistakes," she said. "There will be good, some reason in all this, even if we can't think of any right now."

They began to talk, in soft whispers at first, with frequent bursts of tears, but gradually the tears subsided and the praise became more positive. There was even an occasional chuckle as someone recalled a funny incident from Willie's

life. Soon the whole atmosphere of the room had changed.
Mrs. Corbin had stopped rocking and moaning, and Mr. Corbin was no longer pacing. Someone brought the family Bible
and they began to read, passing the precious book from hand
to hand as they shared its truths.

Later, when I left for home, the Corbin family was still
grieving, but each member had found a source of comfort
beyond themselves.

I waited a day or two before I called on Mrs. Foggelson.
I didn't think I could manage it earlier. I still felt a dull ache
deep within me, and I was afraid if I tried to talk about Willie
I would break up again.

Mrs. Foggelson met me at the door. "Oh, Josh!" she said
with a little cry and she moved quickly toward me, her arms
outstretched.

I held her for a few minutes. She was crying against my
shoulder, but when she moved back she quickly whisked
away the tears and motioned me to the sofa.

We talked about Willie for a long time; we both needed
it. I asked about Camellia.

"How is she?" I asked.

"Crushed!" said Mrs. Foggleson. "Crushed—but she'll
make it. We've talked on the telephone a couple of times."

"When will she be home?"

"Today. On the afternoon train. That was the soonest she
could come."

There was a pause; then she added, "It seems like such a
long way to come for such a short time, but we both felt it
important that she be here for the Memorial Service."

"Short time? What do you mean?"

"She has to go back right away. She's writing important
exams next week."

"You mean she's going to stay on in school?" I couldn't
believe it. Why? Willie was no longer there to draw Camellia
to South Africa.

Of course, I reasoned, *Camellia would not want to quit*

classes halfway through a year. I admired her for that. *But she quit the Interior Design course before she had completed it.* I was puzzled, unable to understand the difference.

"If she doesn't write these exams, she loses a whole semester. That would set her back considerably."

I nodded, a bit surprised that Camellia still wanted to be a nurse.

I went with Mrs. Foggelson to meet Camellia's train. Some of the Corbin family were there as well. There were more tears. Camellia went from one to another, being held and comforted. When it was my turn there was nothing that we could say to each other. I just held her and let her weep, and my heart nearly broke all over again. The three of us walked on home through the chill winter air and Mrs. Foggelson set about making us all a pot of tea.

"Your ma says you need to go back soon," I said to Camellia.

She nodded slowly, a weary hand brushing back her curls.

"You're still set on nursing?"

"Willie said that is the biggest need out there—and who knows? If there had been a nurse there, Willie might not have died."

I could understand that much but not what it had to do with her situation.

"I just wish I hadn't wasted so much time," she went on as though talking to herself. "If I had started my training at the same time Willie did . . ." She left the statement hanging.

"But you didn't know."

"No, I didn't know." Her tone was tired, empty; then she smiled softly. "But at least I'll have the joy of serving the people that Willie learned to love."

It finally got through to me then. Camellia was still planning on going to Africa.

"You're going to go after *this*?" It seemed out of the question.

"Of course," she said simply, as though I shouldn't even need to ask. "They need me."

Chapter 27

God's Call

The three of us made it through the Memorial Service; Mrs. Foggelson asked me to sit with her and Camellia. And then we saw Camellia off on the train again. She held her mother a long, long time as the tears flowed.

"Mamma, I love you so much," she sobbed. "If I didn't *have* to go, I'd stay with you—you know that."

Mrs. Foggelson seemed to understand. She looked Camellia straight in the eyes and said earnestly, "Remember—always, always stand true to your convictions, to what the Lord is telling you."

They hugged one another again, and then Camellia turned to me.

"Thank you, Josh, for always being there. For being such a dear, dear friend to Willie and me." I couldn't say anything in reply. I just held her for a brief moment and then let her go.

I was restless over the next several days. I couldn't seem to think, to sleep, I didn't care to eat—I couldn't even really concentrate when I prayed. My prayers were all broken sentences, pleas of isolated words, fragments of thoughts.

I walked through the days in a stupor. I went through the motions of chores each day. The animals were cared for. Chester got his daily massage and exercise. I moved. I functioned. I spoke. Occasionally I even heard myself laugh, but it was as though another person were existing in my body.

I had to make a trip to town. We needed some groceries and the whole household seemed anxious for a new set of papers.

I went the usual route, picked up the papers at the post office, shuffled through the mail, and my eyes lighted up as they fell on an envelope from South Africa. It was from *Willie*! And then my whole body went numb.

But Willie is dead! Willie is no longer in South Africa!

I looked at the postmark. It was dated several weeks back. Somewhere the letter had been held up.

I put the letter in my coat pocket, *I wonder if I'll even be able to read it,* I thought. But at the same time I knew that there was no way on earth I could keep from reading it.

I didn't open the letter until after I had arrived home, cared for the team, done the chores, had my supper, and retired for the night. I didn't tell anyone about it either—I wasn't sure how its contents were going to affect me.

At last I opened it slowly and let my eyes drift over the familiar script. My hands were shaking as I held the pages to the light of the kerosene lamp.

Willie, in the usual fashion, wrote about the people he was getting to know, how they were learning to trust him and listen when he talked to them about Jesus. His love showed in every word he spoke. You could tell Willie was happy that God had called him to South Africa.

He made comments about my last letter and asked questions about my family and the community. He sent his love to Mary and even teased me a bit about having *two* eligible young ladies in the household.

Then he began to talk about Camellia. *How happy and blessed I am that God brought us together! I always cared for Camellia—right from the first day that she came to our school.*

I watched silently as you and Camellia became friends, both sad and happy at the same time.

And now God has turned everything around; Camellia is going to be my wife. I can hardly believe the way I have been blessed; I hope with all my heart that you haven't been hurt. It will be a long time yet before Camellia can join me; I'm counting every hour, but God is making the busy days pass quickly, and before we know it, she will be at my side.

And then Willie said, *Josh, I don't have to tell you this, but the most exciting thing in the world is to live day by day in the will of God. He has a perfect plan, and if we are obedient to Him He will accomplish it, whether it takes fifty years, twenty years or a single day.*

A sob caught in my throat. I read the paragraph again. Then I went on.

I am thankful that God gave me a good home, a good church, and good friends so that I could learn that truth without fighting it. I know that you have often wondered why the Lord hasn't called you to the pastorate or to the mission field. The important thing isn't where we serve, but how. The question is not "what does He have for me in the future?" but "Am I obedient to Him right now?" And you can walk in obedience, Josh, wherever you live and serve.

May God lead you, Josh, in whatever He has for you. You're the greatest buddy a fellow ever had. Love, Willie.

I cried many tears over that letter. I read it so often in the next several days that I could have repeated it by heart, yet I had a hard time getting to the truth of it.

I was in the barn one morning exercising Chester when the door opened and Uncle Nat came in. After warm greetings, Uncle Nat came over to check out my horse. He was nearly as pleased as I was to see how well Chester was progressing.

"He looks real good, Josh," he said to me. "Soon he'll be running at a full gallop again."

I grinned.

"Well, I sure hope the ice and snow are off the ground before then," I said. "Don't want it to happen again."

"Oh, it will be," said Uncle Nat with confidence.

I shook my head. "Seems to me this winter has hung on and on," I said soberly.

Uncle Nat looked at me evenly. I could read questions in his eyes. He pulled forward a barn stool and sat down.

"So, how's it going, Josh?" I knew that it wasn't just a passing question or a social pleasantry.

I let Chester drift back to his own stall, and I sank onto a soft mound of straw.

"I don't know," I said honestly. "It's been a tough winter."

Uncle Nat nodded.

"Tough times make us grow, Josh," he said simply.

I thought about that. I hoped I had done some growing.

"The farm's doing well," Uncle Nat went on, encouraging me to talk.

"Yeah," I nodded, thinking of the good seed grain in the granaries, the fine stock in the pasture, and the tractor waiting for spring.

"You should be real proud of yourself," Uncle Nat continued. "I know we all are."

"You are? That's good, but I still—"

"You unhappy with farming?" Uncle Nat's question brought me up short.

"Oh no," I was quick to inform him. "I like it—*love* it. It's great to watch things grow—and change—and to know that you've been a part of it."

"But something is bothering you."

"Well, I mean—I still don't know what God wants me to do in life. I expected by now that He would show me, but He hasn't yet. By the time a fella is past twenty-two, he should have some clear direction about his life, he should know what he's supposed to do."

Uncle Nat gave me a playful poke on the arm. "I thought

maybe you had girl troubles," he teased. "Couldn't make up your mind about which one of those fine ladies—"

"Naw," I answered, "not girl troubles." But I pondered Uncle Nat's words.

"I wouldn't even dare to choose a girl now," I added defensively. "Not 'til I know what God has in mind for my life."

"I see," said Uncle Nat.

We were both silent for a few minutes.

"But you enjoy farming?" said Uncle Nat, as though to clear up a point. "You don't feel any kind of guilt for being here for the last several years?"

"I *had* to be here," I said, surprised that Uncle Nat didn't understand that. "Grandpa and Uncle Charlie needed me. There was no one else to help them."

"And with your hard work and good management you have turned the farm around—it's better now than ever."

I appreciated Uncle Nat's lofty compliments, and I had to admit that there was some truth in what he said.

"And you think that the two men will be able to handle the farm now by themselves?"

It was a foolish question. Anyone could see that Grandpa and Uncle Charlie wouldn't do much farming in the future.

"You know they couldn't," I said rather abruptly.

"So they still need you?" Uncle Nat left the question hanging in the air between us. I didn't even try to answer it.

"Have you ever considered the fact that God might want you to go on farming? That farming might be His call for you?"

"*Farming?*" I paused for quite a while. Then I said, "Not really. I just supposed—" I shook my head.

"But you do enjoy farming?" pressed Uncle Nat.

"Sure I do. But it all seems kind of pointless. I've been trying hard to build up the farm so that it would be productive, make money." I lowered my head and picked absently at some straw. "I had even promised God that the money I made would be used to support missionaries—like Willie.

And now—now it all seems wasted." My speech ended with a sob caught in my throat. Uncle Nat sat silently for several minutes until he could see that I had control of myself again.

"I suppose Willie's early death seems a waste to you, too, Josh."

Uncle Nat had tied up my confused feelings into a neat package. I said nothing.

"I don't understand about Willie's death," went on Uncle Nat. "It is sad and it causes us all much pain, but it wasn't wasteful. God doesn't make mistakes, Josh."

"That's what SueAnn said the day we got word of his death. But, Uncle Nat, that's really hard for me to swallow. Look at Willie—if anybody was being faithful to God, he was. So why did God let him die like that, so young, with so much ahead of him?"

Uncle Nat looked intently at me. "Josh, none of us can know for certain *why* these things happen. We may never know. Because God gave man a free will and he chose to sin, we now live in a world marred by sin—"

"But Jesus' death sets us free from sin!" I protested.

"As individuals who trust Him—yes. From the *judgment* of sin. But as long as we live on this earth, we will have to live with the effects of sin."

"Like evil?"

"Evil, and sickness, and accidents, and untimely death— all those things that don't quite seem fair. We live in a sin-damaged world, Josh. People do get sick and die. We may not understand it, but we do know—"

"That God loves us and wants the best for us," I finished for him. Somewhere, in the darkness of my grief and confusion, I felt a light beginning to dawn.

"We have to believe that or life has no meaning," Uncle Nat agreed in a soft, firm voice.

"Now, I don't know the reason for what happened. But there is a purpose. God can make 'all things work together for good'—those aren't just words, Josh. I'm sure of that.

Willie's life accomplished what it was meant to accomplish. Willie was obedient to God. He was right where God wanted Him to be at the time that God wanted him to be there. He wasn't running away; he wasn't fighting God's plan. He was obedient. God can always—and only—fulfill His plan for us when we obey Him—about the daily decisions and the big ones."

Parts of Willie's letter flashed back into my mind. That was what Willie was trying to tell me. All that was really important was that I obey God now, this very moment, at this very place. Tomorrow could be left in God's hands.

Uncle Nat was talking again. "Do you feel that you are disobeying God in farming, Josh?"

"No," I was able to answer honestly. "I really don't."

"Then if you are not disobeying Him, could it be that you are *obeying* Him?"

I stared at Uncle Nat, thinking. Then I began to chuckle. "It seems so simple," I said, tossing a handful of straw into the air.

"Maybe it is. Maybe we're the ones who make it complicated."

I felt as if a great burden had suddenly been lifted from my shoulders. Uncle Nat and I hugged each other and then he held me away and said softly, "Josh, there are other missionaries who will still need to be supported. Camellia, for one."

Tears filled my eyes. I guess there was no other missionary I would rather support than Willie's Camellia. I nodded, too choked up to speak.

"You ready to go?" asked Uncle Nat.

I was ready all right. I had been spending too much of my time hidden away in the barn lately. Chester was doing just fine on his own. He didn't need me that much anymore. *At least for now, God wants me to be a farmer—the best one possible,* I thought. *Unless or until He shows me something else* . . . And I had the big issue settled. I was ready to get on with some of the other decisions that a fellow has to make. I gave Uncle Nat a smile—the first in a long time, it seemed. We left the barn and I fastened the door securely behind me.

As we headed for the house, I lifted my eyes to study the farm I loved. A distinct feeling of spring filled the morning air.